BURN

Naomi Charles

Burn
Copyright © 2022 by Naomi Charles

First paperback edition November 2022

Cover art and design by Okay Creations
ISBN 978-1-7352292-5-3

Prologue

Once upon a time, there was a girl who was in love. She was in love with a prince. She was so in love that everyday, she would wait where he walked so that one day, he would finally notice her. He finally did. They walked together in the kingdom and everyone wished they were the girl, or what everyone soon called the lucky girl. Everyone thought she would become a princess.

Then one day, the prince seemed different. He would be late to their walks around their kingdom. He seemed distracted, and the lucky girl became worried. When she would ask the prince what the problem was, he would say that he was fine. Still, the lucky girl knew something was wrong.

It wasn't until it was too late that the lucky girl found out what had happened to the prince. When she finished her performance with the other noble women of the land, she noticed that no one was paying attention to her at all. Instead, all the people were looking at someone else—another girl who stood beside the prince. The prince had decided to make someone else his princess.

At first, the one lucky girl, now just the girl, wondered why it was not her he had chosen. Why would he embarrass her in this way? Then, she heard the rumors of the land. The girl was not considered beautiful enough. She did not have the loose curls, the fair skin, and the blue eyes that the new princess had. She was deep bronze with hair that would stand up to greet the sun, and while she was beautiful, she, apparently, was not beautiful enough. And what made it worse was that it seemed that most people in the land agreed.

Chapter 1

Rachel

For as long as I can remember, I've lived by the philosophy of balance. For every up, there is a down. For all the bad, there is an equal amount of good. For all the ice, there will be fire. You get it. This philosophy had always been foolproof, and I openly swore by it. I didn't need the fancy religious rules some people were into. I was all about *Rachel's Bad Bitch Book of Balance*—copyright around the time I was old enough to think.

I'll even give you some examples. For all the absolute garbage life has thrown my sister, she was granted with undoubted beauty, a gorgeous man for a boyfriend (yes, I hate him, but I'm not blind), a marriage that ensured that she would be swimming in billions until she died, and power. My father grew up in the system and bounced from house to house when he was a kid, but he got so many scholarships he never had to pay for college, eventually became a doctor, and was married to the love of his life, my mother. Jason almost got killed when he meddled in The Table's schemes, but he was able to find his brother that he had been looking for for years. Eliza's life looked like it sucked too, but at least she looked like a model and was filthy rich. See? Balance.

It seemed like everyone got that nice balance except me. I'm not saying I didn't have my wins and losses, but they were certainly not balanced. What I got in turn for my grief was very lackluster, and all I wanted were a few wins to make it all worth it. I figured that I would finally find one of those wins once I got to college, but nothing. And when I saw Noah Crawford, my brother-in-law, walking on my campus, the place where I felt free from the baggage each of us accumulated in the previous year, I knew I was probably going to experience another loss instead of a win.

He swaggered in my direction across the football field where the dance team practiced before the football team did. Everyone stopped and looked at him as if he owned the universe. I rolled my eyes and crossed my arms when he stopped only a few yards away.

"What is it, Crawford?" I asked loud enough for him to hear me.

"I need to talk to you," he said in a low voice only I could hear.

"Where's Nicole?" I asked.

"She's in New York at a meeting that I should be at, but I need to speak to you," he said, and I immediately felt my stomach tighten.

"This is my last practice before the game tonight," I said.

"Then I'll wait here." He shrugged.

I sighed and glanced at my friend Ash, who was looking at me curiously. Not the kind of curiosity that she usually gave me around guys, since she knew Nicole and Noah were married, but the type where she knew something was up. I lifted a shoulder, more to show that it's an annoying manner than anything else, and she finally looked away. Ashlyn and I both made it onto Temple University's dance team and just like that, our days of dancing on a team together were extended for another four years.

"Twenty minutes. That's how long you have to wait," I said before I walked back to the team.

Instead of going back to sit in his car like a normal person, Noah sat on the bleachers nearby. Of course, a lot of the girls were distracted by his presence. As long as no one got hurt before the performance, I didn't care. We wrapped up, and everyone watched as I walked off the field. I waited for a few seconds before I started asking questions.

"What do you want, Crawford?" I asked.

"There's an issue with security," Noah sighed.

"When is there *not*? Aren't they looking for Josh? No offense, but what does that have to do with me? Does this pose any extra threat to Nicole?" I asked.

"No… Actually, we don't know yet," he said.

"Okay, so why are we having this conversation?" I asked.

"Greg thinks something is coming. I want you to lay low and be careful," he said.

"Define laying low."

"Being aware of your surroundings… Not going to large events," he went on.

I stopped walking, and he paused just a few steps ahead of me. He gave me a questioning look, raising a brow. This white man really thought he was going to tell me to not go to public events during my freshman year of college. I laughed.

"What?" he asked.

"That's not going to work for me. I have things to do," I said.

"What's more important than staying alive?"

"Being alive with good memories; memories that you're not ruining," I added.

"I'm not here to ruin anything," Noah sighed.

"Yes, I know, but you do that anyway, Crawford," I shouted over my shoulder as I walked toward my car in the lot.

"So you're not going to hear what I have to say? You're just going to continue as usual?" He called after me as I walked away.

"I want to live life normally for once, especially here. I haven't done that in months because of your shit. I missed out on my senior year of high school," I said before I got in my car.

Chapter 2

Rachel

I'd just finished showering when the R&B music playing from my phone was interrupted by an incoming call. I tapped the screen without looking and answered it on speaker. I asked who it was, and I heard a distinct voice on the other end. It was always friendly, no matter the situation, and was smooth. For some reason, I always thought of warm milk chocolate whenever I heard him speak. There was richness. A sweetness. Just slightly mysterious, but mostly straight forward. He always sounded like he was on the verge of laughter—that was the sweet part, but he also always sounded like he had you all figured out already—-that was the mysterious part. It was usually pretty comforting to hear, even if what was being said was often annoying. I mean, how could he not have annoying traits when he was pretty much a combination of Jason Westbrook and Noah Crawford? Poor man had the universe working against him on that one.

"It's me wondering how college taught you to *not* use common sense." Josh chuckled.

"Don't start, Joshua. I already heard from your brother today," I said.

"What does that have to do with anything?" he scoffed.

"I can only take so much Crawford crap in one day," I retorted.

Josh didn't say anything, but I could pretty much hear him rolling his eyes. I rolled mine back as I rubbed cocoa butter into my skin quickly. I didn't have much time before I needed to be at the game.

"I know you have a game, so I will only annoy you for ten minutes," he said.

"Why do you deserve ten *whole* minutes of my time?" I asked.

"Because we're team-in-law, Ray. It's our weekly meeting. Keep up," he sighed as if I should have known this. We came up with that team name when we decided to step in and make sure Nicole and Noah didn't get a divorce. Seemed like a monumentally bad idea for the both of them.

"Josh, can this wait? I have to get to the game in less than an hour, and I haven't done my makeup or hair yet. My whole ass is going to be late right now," I said, throwing on some fresh undergarments.

"*Your whole ass*? As opposed to half or one-seventh of it?" he began, and I let out a loud groan, trying not to laugh in frustration.

"This is why I hang up on you!" I yelled.

"Fine, I'm just calling to tell you to be careful. Seriously. Noah is pretty worried about it, and he's not really saying why. But if you think of it, everyone has been targeted, even in a minor way, besides you and myself," he said.

"I'll be fine. I'm always fine."

I *was* fine, and the dance team went to Pat's, a local bar, to celebrate after. Some of the girls were on the dance floor, but Ash and I didn't feel like it this time. We sat on a couple bar stools and nursed a couple drinks. I was sitting, people-watching, when I noticed my friend gazing at me in my peripheral vision. I turned to her slowly.

"What was up today?" Ash asked, and I already knew what she was referring to without having to ask.

"Just Noah being annoying. It's nothing." I shrugged.

"He came all the way to Philadelphia to be annoying?" She was clearly inferring that there was more to the story.

Ashlyn didn't know much about what had happened in my life over the past year. It was clear she wanted to know, but she respected my boundaries. The only thing she knew was that Noah and Nicole were married. She had drunk the Nicole and Noah kool-aid back when they still went to Jefferson. It was hard not to. They were the perfect couple, until they weren't. Nicole was a phenomenal cheerleader, student, and everything else. Noah was the mysterious, pretty boy every girl coveted. When she heard that they had tied the knot, she celebrated first and asked questions after… barely.

"No, he was in town and decided to annoy me." I took a sip of my drink, shifting my focus back to the floor.

Ash shook her head, a sign she was getting tired of not getting the answers she wanted. I was off the hook for now, I thought. She took another sip of her drink before her head snapped back to me again. I sighed deeply in her direction.

"What?" I asked.

"Does that mean his *gorgeous* brother is in town?" she asked.

"Who? Josh? No, he's in Queens," I said dryly.

Ashlyn was the biggest fan of Josh. According to her, he was "top-tier" as far as the good-looking department went. She had seen him a few times during the summer when Noah could convince him to come down to the city, and it was apparent that she had a major crush. Ash's twin sister, Angelica, actually agreed that he was a top-tier guy, which was shocking since she had said many times that "all men were the scum of the Earth," and that was the reason why she decided to date girls. To me, Josh was just my annoying extended family member that I played video games with and helped navigate the social aspects of life.

"That's a shame. How is he?" she asked.

"He's fine. I mean, he's Josh."

"He should come visit us," Ash said excitedly.

"I'd rather dip my toe in hot acid," I deadpanned.

"You're no fun," she frowned.

"And neither is he," I said.

Ash didn't respond to my comment and instead looked behind me. Her eyes started to widen, and I felt a knot begin to form in my stomach. Like my sister, I wasn't very fond of surprises—especially lately with how life had decided to be. I slowly turned around to see Kadeem White walking in my direction. He was looking right at me, and my mind began to calculate all the reasons why that would be.

"Rachel," he said when he got close enough.

"Kadeem," I greeted him in the same fashion.

"I'm going to run to the ladies room," Ash said, as she slid out of her chair and disappeared into the crowd.

Kadeem pointed to the now vacant chair with questioning eyes. I nodded reluctantly, and he sat. I was trying to appear as unbothered as possible, but I didn't have much prep time.

"How can I help you?" I asked before sipping my drink.

"I saw you at halftime today. You looked great," he said.

No shit, of course I did. Try harder, White.

"Thank you," I said, offering no handouts for the conversation to go any further.

"I've also wanted to reach out to you for a while but just didn't know how to go about it. I feel like we got off on the wrong foot," he said, putting his finger up for a waiter.

"If that's what you'd like to call it," I snorted.

"Two more of whatever she's having," he said to the waiter before turning to me.

"Where's Taylor?" I asked.

"Somewhere… I haven't seen her much lately," he shrugged uneasily.

"Interesting, you know, Kadeem, the last time you said that she came back," I said, not even attempting to feign interest.

"That was high school."

"*That* was just seven months ago. You left me dateless for prom. Why the hell should I even talk to you?" I asked, grabbing one of the drinks the waiter brought.

"We were great together. I think Taylor and I just needed some closure. I don't think you'd want to be in that mix anyway," he said.

"So what do you want now?"

"Let me take you out somewhere nice."

***

It was halftime, and the school band was playing as the dance team ran out onto the field. The high school crowd cheered as we assembled into formation for the last time of the year. I looked out into the bleachers to see my parents waving. Nicole, Noah, and Josh stood there too, but something was wrong. Nicole was smiling like everyone else, but her smile seemed strained. *Don't think about it until after, Rach,* I told myself. The band's music was interrupted by a pop remix that started to play from the sound system. I decided to look elsewhere to distract myself from my sister's expression.

We began to move in unison, and the crowd roared. I smiled— that feeling would never get old. My first flip was coming up. I took a deep breath and stuck the landing. I could hear my parents scream the loudest. I laughed and continued in a few spins. The second row slid forward ahead of mine when the song changed. We did a few illusions. When I looked back out into the crowd, I saw Josh and Noah no longer smiling either. Josh's gaze was fixed on me, and I looked down quickly to make sure I didn't have a wardrobe malfunction. I didn't. What was the problem?

The team was ready for the final move which was a split leap. We did the last complicated steps and stuck the landing after our jump. The crowd cheered. We finally left our positions and started to wave. I looked into the crowd and that's when I saw Taylor Morris. I saw her making out with Kadeem. My Kadeem. She was sitting in his lap kissing him. I stopped waving and froze immediately.

"What's wrong?" Ashlyn walked over and put her arm around me.

I didn't answer. Instead, I walked over to the two without even thinking of what I would do when I got there. Taylor noticed first and started smiling triumphantly. Kadeem noticed second, and he went from smiling to grimacing, afraid.

"Oh, Rachel. Hi," he said.

"What are you doing?" I asked.

"Aw, poor thing. Kay, you didn't tell her yet?" Taylor asked mockingly.

"Tell me what?" I asked.

"We got back together," Kadeem said nervously.

I was silent and stayed still. If I didn't, I would've killed them both. People started to watch, and I couldn't help but feel embarrassed. I willed myself not to dare cry in front of them, especially not in front of Taylor. She hated me, though I never knew why. I just knew she always got away with the worst shit because everyone thought she was pretty with her long brown hair and light skin. It wasn't fair she got to have everything when she quite literally was a complete and utter bitch.

"Let's go, Rachel," I heard Nicole's voice next to me.

"Oh my God, Nicole! Uh, hi! You're back from NYU," Taylor gushed.

Nicole rolled her eyes at the obvious fan of hers and pulled me away. She pulled me to the parking lot and only when we got to the car did I let out the scream begging to be let free out of my lungs.

After that night, Khadeem tried to apologize on multiple occasions. He failed each time. The stories about him making a poor judgment in sitting next to Taylor during halftime and still being confused how he felt about her did not do the job of making me feel better. We didn't speak for the rest of the school year.

***

Until now. There was no question I was still attracted to the guy. Tall, dark, and covered in some gorgeous muscles. He had the most perfect smile that could make anybody melt. Equipped with the weapons to make anyone defenseless. In fact, he was using it on me now.

"If you really want to go on a date with me, because that is what you're asking, right? Ask me tomorrow when you haven't been drinking and you're no longer trying to score for the night," I said and walked away.

Chapter 3

Josh

I watched Noah's stone-like expression as he decided whether he was going to go for my bait in our chess game. He was trying to figure out if I was trapping him. Thing was, the only person who could keep a straight face better than him was me. He moved the exact piece I expected him to. I let a smile creep up one side of my face. I moved my knight and captured his king, winning the game. He groaned and sat back.

"This isn't over." Noah chuckled.

"You know where to find me if you'd like to redeem yourself," I teased.

"You're on… once I figure out more about what's going on," he sighed.

"Yeah, Rachel told me you showed up in Philly last week," I said, reorganizing my chess pieces.

"I'm sure she expressed her discontentment. I just want her to be mindful. I get that she doesn't want to have any part of this."

"Isn't Tracey looking for me? What would Rachel have to worry about in Pennsylvania?"

"She's important to Nicole, and my mother hates Nicole, so while you need to be careful, she does too."

"That's fair," I said.

We heard the dings of the elevator that led to the penthouse apartment. Noah looked up and I turned to see Nicole walk through the parting doors. She looked like she had walked off the set of a high-budget workplace drama. Her flowy deep gold top matched her shoes. Her skirt was formed around her like it was made specifically for her body. She walked in with so much confidence that one would probably feel scared if they didn't know her. She gave me a small smile before her husband wrapped her in his arms and gave her a long kiss.

"How are you?" Noah asked, grabbing her coat from her hand.

"Okay," she sighed.

"Just okay?" he questioned further.

"Well, Mr. Elliott was not pleased with some of the changes I decided to make. He made getting through the meeting very difficult," she said as she stepped out of her shoes.

"Who's Mr. Elliot?" Noah asked.

"The man you refer to as Bow Tie," she said.

"Oh. That annoying fuck face," he grumbled.

"He doesn't understand why the rules must change. I mentioned the fact that killing people is not our way and he said that *you* would understand when you're older. I, on the other hand, may not because I'm a woman," she scoffed.

"That's so embarrassing," I remarked.

"So embarrassing! He's stuck in the wrong century," Nicole agreed as she walked over and gave me a one-arm hug around my neck.

"I'm sorry I couldn't be there today. I had to smile and shake hands at some benefit after class," Noah said.

"That's okay. I don't mind flipping the patriarchy on its head a couple times a week." Nicole grinned.

"You sound like Rachel," I said.

"That reminds me, she should be home for Thanksgiving in a few days. Mom wanted to know if you would join the rest of us for dinner that night?" Nicole asked softly.

"Sure." I answered with a smile, grateful that the Smiths were so kind to me. They oozed family and love and all I wanted to do was absorb as much as they were willing to extend my way.

I felt my phone vibrate in my pocket. I slid it out of my pocket and looked at the screen. "Erica (Mom)" lit up on my screen. She wanted to video chat. I sighed because if there was something that I despised more than unannounced visitors was being video called without a warning text. Excusing myself, I went into the guest room I was staying in and answered. My mother showed up on the screen with a smile that rivaled the sun. I flashed her a small smile back.

"Joshua, how are you?" she asked.

"I'm alright. How are you?" I asked, though I was not in the mood for small talk. I never was.

"Good. I just wanted to check in and see how you were. How's Noah? You said you were in Queens for a few weeks right?"

"Noah's doing well. He's spending some time with Nicole. She just got home."

"Yes, the perfect couple. I'm happy they found each other and stayed together at such a young age. That doesn't happen often," she said, and I could hear a trace of heartache in her voice.

I wasn't sure if I would consider Nicole and Noah the perfect couple. They sure did have pretty hectic lives. Yet, I'm not sure if I could see either of them with someone else. I knew Nicole had dated Jason, and Noah had dated Eliza, but something just seemed so wrong about all of that. They also did look quite immaculate together.

Maybe they *were* the perfect couple. I mean, what did I know? I didn't have the slightest clue about love.

"I'm glad they're happy. They deserve it," I finally said.

"What are you going to do while in the city? I want you to be careful, but you should have fun too. Maybe you'll meet someone there," she said.

"Nothing much. Noah likes to keep an eye on me when he can't visit upstate often because of school. I've been fine this whole time, but I decided it would be nice to escape all the snow. Maybe I'll go to Manhattan to see the Christmas stuff in a few weeks." I decided to ignore the "meeting someone" part.

"Family is important," she replied, and I used every muscle in my body to resist rolling my eyes.

I never questioned it, but I figured out very early that Erica had probably known I was alive and decided to not look for me. She knew too much and seemed too unfazed from the fact I was now alive and in her world. I think the fact that she was my mother made the whole thing too tiresome to try to unpack. There was definitely a monumental amount of things *to* unpack, though.

"Yes, I know. I just like my space. I thrive off of it," I insisted.

"Well, I will let you go. Call me soon. I love hearing from you. I love you."

"Love you too, Mom," I replied before hanging up.

The Wednesday before Thanksgiving was hectic, and Noah and I weren't even the ones cooking. Noah was stressed because he was hyper focused on pleasing the Smiths. I'm not sure why he thought making sure he was impeccably manicured was going to achieve that. Nonetheless, he made sure his hair was cut, face was clean shaven, and his clothes for the next day were wrinkleless.

"Remind me again. Why do you think being annoyingly polished is going to make them think you're not a murderer?" I asked as I watched my brother slowly lose himself into idiocy.

"I don't know. I need to do something, don't I? By the way, you should freshen up too," he added, and I looked over at myself in the mirror.

"It's too late to get a barber," I said, patting my overgrown hair and frowning at my not-so-shadow-anymore beard.

"No, it's not. I know someone. Also, you should keep the new beard and just clean it up." He nodded in approval before putting his phone to his ear and walking down his hall.

Within an hour, my hair was cut and my beard was figured out. When the barber finished, he handed me a mirror, and I almost didn't recognize myself. He had cut a lot off. I was surprised I didn't hate it. The barber waited for my approval, which I finally gave with a smile and a nod.

"A little change is always good," the man said. He wasn't wrong.

"Thanks," I agreed.

The next day, Noah drove us to the Smiths'. He had his typical hard expression, but it was laced with the chaotic energy he was giving off.

"It's going to be fine. You dated Nicole before. They know you. It's not like you're telling them you're married," I said.

"Shit. I have to take off my wedding band. I left it on," he swore, wiggling it off and handing it to me.

"Thanks, you shouldn't have," I deadpanned.

"Just hold it for me," he sighed.

I rolled my eyes as I put it in my pocket. And yes, just in case you were wondering, he did have pockets too. I turned to look out the window to see all the perfect homes go by. I saw families going for walks and children riding their bikes through leaf piles. Normal stuff. It was crazy to think that I was born in a world like this one when I was barely part of it. I always wondered if my lack of experience immediately made me stand out to people. The past almost-year gave me the answer to that, which was that no one cared enough to notice, but it still came up in my thoughts from time-to-time.

***

I stared at the little chandelier that hung from the ceiling in Rachel's bedroom. It was later in the afternoon, and the sun rays sneaking through her blinds turned the crystals into little prisms. I found myself distracted by the little rainbows that illuminated the room.

"I'm so glad you agree," Rachel said, pulling me out of my train of thought.

"What?" I asked, sitting up, to see my feet next to her.

"I said to stay silent if you agree and you stayed silent." She crossed her arms with a devious smile.

I rolled my eyes and put my foot near her face, threatening to touch my toe to her cheek. She picked up a pillow and held it up, threatening to hit me. Ah, family. I put my foot down as a sign of peace.

"Okay, I retreat. Please, no more abuse. I carried so many bags today when you were shopping for prom crap," I mock-cried.

"I told you that you didn't have to! I easily could've carried them or put some in my trunk," she retorted.

"Well, is that the gentleman thing to do? Carry bags and stuff?" I asked.

She paused and gave me a weary look. Then a long exhale sounded from her.

"You worry me sometimes," she sighed.

"Why?" I asked.

"Because you're so good, so innocent. I worry that some girl is going to take advantage of you."

"That won't happen. I would see it coming. She wouldn't know I'm like this until I get to know her."

"You don't hide that part of yourself well," she pointed out.

"Yes I do. I show you because we're friends," I argued.

"No, you don't. I noticed it in a day and so did my friends," she said as she reached for her frappuccino cup to take a sip.

"I didn't know it was that obvious." I scratched the back of my head.

"Well, that's why I'm here. By the time *Project Swaggy Josh* is over, no one will know you didn't grow up with other kids around," she said, and I felt myself cringe.

"We are *not* naming it that.".

***

When we got to the house, Noah exhaled heavily before leaving the car, looking as if he didn't care about anything. It was a talent how he did that. I followed him to the door. Nicole opened it with a warm smile. Noah kissed her forehead, and she gave me a once over before she nodded in approval.

"I like it. You look very distinguished," she said before giving me a hug.

"Thanks. By the way, I finished the book," I added.

"Ooh, we have to chat about it soon!" She clasped her hands excitedly.

Rachel walked down the stairs with a curious gaze pointed in my direction. I nodded to greet her when she got to the bottom of the stairs.

"What's going on with your face, Joshy?" she asked.

"What do you mean? I got a haircut," I hesitated, not expecting that to be her response.

"Rachel, be nice," Nicole warned from Noah's arms.

"I didn't say he looked bad. He just looks different," she sighed, giving Nicole a bored glare.

"I'll take that as a raving compliment," I said.

Just then, Mr. and Mrs. Smith came walking from the kitchen. Mr. Smith gave Noah a hug, and as they exchanged a few words about sports, Mrs. Smith wrapped her arms around me without warning. Her embrace was so warm and genuine. I gave her a smile.

"Joshua, how are you? You look so handsome," she beamed with my face between her hands.

"Thanks, Mrs. Smith, and I'm doing well." I chuckled.

"Jaz, give the boy some air. How are you, son?" Mr. Smith asked, giving me the same hug he gave Noah.

"I'm doing well, sir," I greeted.

"I'm glad you're here, Joshua. I want to show you something," Mrs. Smith said, not allowing a moment for things to get quiet.

I started to follow her as she happily skipped to the kitchen. I heard Rachel scoff.

"Mom, he does not care about your high-tech spice rack," Rachel groaned.

"Speak for yourself, Ray Ray. I'm intrigued," I said, looking over my shoulder before reaching the kitchen.

I could see Rachel roll her eyes at the nickname, but she still smiled.

Chapter 4

Rachel

Noah non-verbally insisted on sitting next to Nicole by refusing to let go of her hand as if she were his life source right before we sat down. That meant I had to sit next to Josh.

"Oh hey, it's my buddy," Josh teased softly as I settled in the chair next to him.

I didn't answer with words, but instead an incredulous glance and small shake of my head. He smiled anyway before we all bowed our heads during Dad's prayer.

At first, we passed around plates of different sides. It was clear that we were all starving and had no interest in conversation unless it involved asking for something to be passed until our plates were hidden with food piled on top of it. Once that was over, it became silent again. That was until my lovely sister decided to break the ice at my expense.

"So since we did this to me when I first came home from school, I've decided to continue the tradition," Nicole began.

"What?" I asked.

"Meet anyone at school?" Nicole asked conspiratorially.

Everyone at the tables oohed and ahhed. I began to think of the ways I would get back at my sister while simultaneously thinking of how to answer. Yes, I did meet a couple guys, but not anyone they needed to know about. They weren't serious. The only notable person was Kadeem.

"Not really. Speaking of, I saw Kadeem the other day after the game," I said nonchalantly.

Josh turned to me slowly with a disapproving grimace that created little lines between his eyebrows. *What was his problem? Why would he even have an opinion on this?*

"Kadeem White? The guy you almost went to prom with?" Nicole asked, mouth agape.

"Gee, thanks for reminding me, Nicole. It's not like I remember not going to prom," I bit back.

"Okay, okay, I was just asking. He sounded like a jerk anyway," Nicole sighed.

"He's not, just a typical man." I was almost surprised I was defending him.

"Alright, let's not do this at the table. I'd like to digest the fruits of my labor without the sound of my daughters arguing," Dad insisted.

"Good thing this isn't fruit," I mumbled under my breath. It was a risky comment to make, but he gave me a wry smile.

I glanced across the table again and noticed Noah was staring at Josh intently with a questioning raise of a brow. In my peripheral vision, Josh held a stoic stare back, radiating discomfort.

"What's the matter?" I glanced at both of them.

"Nothing, but I'm confused on why you're lending any time to a complete idiot," Josh said in a bored tone.

"He's not an idiot," I defended.

"I have direct evidence to prove this guy is an idiot," Josh answered.

"Hey, listen guys, Rachel can date whoever she wants… even if he is a loser," Noah interjected, and I wanted to flip him the finger for not being helpful.

"Well, not *whoever* she wants," Dad warned.

"Yes, but someone worth your time," Mom agreed.

If there was something that I really hated, it was being told what to do. I always handled my shit, so was there a need for anyone to feel as if they needed to patronize me? The answer was no, just in case that wasn't clear. Everyone was still adding their comments when I dropped my utensils with a loud clang. The chaos paused.

"Nicole, next time you want to ask about my love life in front of everyone, don't. Everyone else, thanks, but I didn't ask for your opinions. I'd like to enjoy my time being back here, please. The last time I was here I had to deal with everyone feeling bad about what happened with prom. I'm tired of it," I announced.

"Rachel, relax, it's not like——" Nicole began condescendingly.

"What is not like, Nicole? Hm? Is it not like getting married behind Mom and Dad's backs to your murder suspect boyfriend? *You're right*, it's not, but it's my right to not want to speak about it. Also, don't tell me to relax!".

The room stilled. Nicole's jaw dropped a little as if she couldn't move besides that. Noah dropped his face into his palm. Mom and Dad looked as if they were calculating what I had just said. Josh's eyes didn't dare to meet mine. Instead, he glued his attention to his plate with a pained expression.

"Dude," Josh breathed.

Dad stood up with so much force that his chair fell back with a loud crash. Nicole threw herself in front of

Noah as Dad reached out to grab him. Mom got up and grabbed his arm to calm him down.

"Are you pregnant?" Dad asked through his teeth.

"What?" Noah responded clearly caught off guard by the question, which was a bad idea.

"Boy, I asked if you got my daughter pregnant," Dad roared.

"No, Daddy, I'm not pregnant. Please stop. You're scaring me," Nicole said with tears in her eyes.

"Sir, I love your daughter," Noah said as evenly as he could manage.

"Why could this not wait? You're children," Dad said.

"We didn't want to wait," Noah said.

"Well, you can't stay here. I'm sorry. You have to leave," Mom said, making everyone freeze in place.

"*Who* has to leave?" Nicole asked in a shaky voice.

"Both of you. You want to be so grown? You can't wait? You can be grown out of my house," Mom said, and I wondered if she understood how crazy rich Noah was and how much of a non-financial hardship that would be for them.

Nicole's hands shook as she stood up in disbelief. Noah stood up next to her with a hand on his chest, probably deciphering the best way to reason with my parents.

"Now, Mr. and Mrs. Smith—" Noah began.

"You ruined my daughter's life! She was a shell of who she used to be, and she's never fully been right since. I should have never let you near her again." Dad clenched his fists, nearly shaking from his anger.

"Dad, how could you say that? I've been fine," Nicole choked out.

"No, you are not the same. You've never gone back to how you used to be," he responded.

"Dad, I grew up," Nicole said softly so we wouldn't hear the emotion in her voice.

"Get your things. Get out," Dad demanded.

Nicole exhaled shakily, moving away from the table, but not before giving me a look that I had never received from her before. I opened my mouth to say something, but at that moment, I couldn't.

I watched in silence as Nicole threw things into a couple duffle bags. I didn't know what to say or do. I knew nothing besides the fact that I wanted to take it back. I screwed things up royally.

"Coco, I will fix this," I promised.

"No, you can't," she croaked.

"I will. I'll talk to Dad and—".

"There are some things you can't undo, Rachel. Fucking think before you speak next time," she said before zipping up the bags.

"I didn't mean for this to happen," I whispered.

"Well, that's not going to help anyone is it? I'm leaving." She stood up straight and pushed past me with her bags.

I followed her downstairs. Josh stood at the bottom and took the bags from her when she reached the last step. We locked eyes for a second, and he gave me a sad tip of his head before he turned to leave behind Nicole. I felt tears fighting to leave my eyes as I looked over at Mom as she stared at the door with a tired purse of her lips.

"Mommy, I messed up," I cried.

She didn't say anything. Instead, she let me cry on her shoulder.

I always felt cold whenever I cried. This time wasn't an exception. I wrapped myself in my fluffy blanket and scrolled aimlessly on social media. Usually, this would distract me for a little bit, but this time, it did nothing for me. I switched over to my texts and tried to text Nicole again as I shivered. It had been over an hour, and she had not answered me. A call from Joshua Crawford popped up and I answered.

"How is she?" I asked as soon as I pressed the green button.

"She's decent. She's watching a movie with Noah in the living room now," Josh answered.

"How do I fix this?"

"I… I don't know. What are your parents saying?"

"They went to bed. Both of them haven't said a word in hours, at least not to me."

"Hopefully they are willing to talk in the morning. How are you?"

"I want to throw myself out my window."

"But who will I piss off by existing then?"

"Josh, I'm serious. I really messed up."

"You did, but we will figure this out. We're a team, remember? We stopped Noah and Nicole from getting divorced, and we'll get through this too," he vowed in a tired, but warm and reassuring tone.

Chapter 5

Rachel

For the next couple days, Mom and Dad made it crystal clear that they had no interest in discussing what happened over Thanksgiving dinner. I knew they weren't as upset with me as they were Nicole, but I still felt the ice. Unfortunately, all of this meant that there was zero chance to fix what I had done. When Dad drove me to the train station for my ride back to Philly, I decided to push a little more than I had over the past couple days. Worst case scenario would be that he would get upset and I would leave the car and sit in the station for longer than I planned.

"Dad," I said, interrupting the silence.

"Hmm?"

"I think you should know something."

"And what's that?"

"Nicole would not have married Noah if it weren't for an important reason."

He didn't answer immediately and puffed out a breath as he made a left turn. I patiently waited for him to answer.

"What's so important that she couldn't wait until she finished school?"

"Who knows, but we know Nicole. She *never* makes the bad decisions… That's me. If she felt like this was what she needed to do, I think we should respect that."

"She's so young."

"She is, but she's the most mature nineteen year old that I know. I trust her. I think we all should," I said softly.

"I don't want her to get distracted," he finally replied after a moment of quiet.

If the past year hadn't distracted Nicole then nothing would. School came naturally for her. She could handle being married. She'd already been handling it for the past almost year.

"Dad, she's going to be fine. It's Nicole. Besides, there was a point in time we all thought that those two would end up together," I said.

"That was before everything."

"Will you promise to at least speak to her?"

"When we're ready, your mother and I will speak to her. Until then, we won't," he said firmly, signaling the conversation was over.

When I got back to my dorm, Ang and Ash immediately stopped speaking when they saw my face. I rolled my small suitcase into the common area and pushed the door in behind me.

"Hey," I sighed, making my way to the bedroom.

"Okay, stop right there. What happened to you?" Ang asked, loud and concerned, making me halt.

"I fucked up with my family this weekend," I grumbled.

Ash and Ang exchanged confused looks, the way twins do.

"What happened? You guys are perfect. You guys are literally like… like the Obamas," Ang said.

"You can't say stuff like that, Ang. There are many successful black families, other than the Obamas." Ash jabbed her sister in the side.

"Sorry, Rach. I totally love the Obamas and didn't mean it in a rude way. I know there are many successful black families, but you and Nicole are like the daughters. *Come on*, Ash. Rach is not worried about me being a racist," Ang said, clearly being annoying on purpose to make me laugh.

I snorted and rolled my eyes. Ang gave me a triumphant smile before she spun around to get the popcorn that was finished popping in the microwave. She didn't live in the same dorm room Ash and I lived in. Instead, she had chosen to live in a single room a floor up from us. There was no doubt Ang and Ash loved each other, but I think they hated being compared. The good one, the bad one. I think the space was good for them. Ash rolled her eyes and shook her head. Ashlyn usually followed the straight and narrow. If she had not wanted to be a doctor, she would've been a great politician.

"Do you want to talk about it?" Ash asked, following me into our room.

"No, not right now. I just need some time, and I'll feel better," I said, hanging my coat up on a hook in my closet.

"Okay, well, Ang and I are going out downtown for a few hours. We need to decompress after our weekend," she replied.

"What happened?" I asked.

"It was just our mom talking about us not doing well enough and what will the other families think? You know, the typical Asian household drama." She gestured with her hand, showing that this was nothing new.

"I'm sorry. What did your dad say?" I asked. Mr. Dumas wasn't Asian, but French and Haitian.

"He holds us in high regard too, so he agrees with her," she said.

"Ew, are we speaking about the people who spawned us?" Ang asked, walking into the room.

"Yeah," Ash sighed.

"What do you think they'll do if I end up coming home with a woman?" Ang snorted.

"I don't even want to think about it, honestly." Ash shuddered.

"You better prepare yourself now. Unless someone magical like Joshua Crawford comes around or maybe the man himself." She gleamed a devious smile.

"He's mine," Ash whined.

"What is wrong with you guys?" I finally chimed in.

"We have eyes. You can't tell me you don't see how much of a catch he is," Ang said.

"He's okay, I guess." I shrugged.

"Well it might be different now that he's part of your family through marriage," Ash chimed in.

"I wouldn't care. He's nice, smart, funny, gorgeous, and he's packing where it matters most, the bank account," she sighed adoringly. I quipped an eyebrow up at her, and she laughed.

There was something so soothing about watching the twins go back and forth. Maybe it was because it was so familiar. I had known them since we were five, and when we graduated from kindergarten, they indoctrinated me as their extra sibling. I never had doubts that they loved me. The hardest thing was not telling them about everything that had unfolded the past year. It wasn't that I didn't want to tell them, but I couldn't. I think that's why Josh and I had gotten closer. I didn't have to cut corners in my stories or omit whole parts of my weekend. He could know it all, and that was priceless.

My phone rang, breaking my train of thought and the twins' banter. I looked and saw Kadeem White's name on my screen. Ang raised an eyebrow as I answered it.

"Hello?" I answered.

"Hey, I see you're back on campus. Let me take you out tonight," Kadeem's voice came confidently through the other end of the phone .

"And what if I don't want to go out with you?" I countered.

"Everything you want is my treat, and I mean everything and anything," he said suggestively, making Ash cover her face next to me.

"Hmm, I see. So you're talking free drinks?"

"Mhm, plus whatever else you want."

"And food? Wow you really drive a good bargain, Deem. Alright, I'll see you at my door in thirty minutes."

"See you then." He chuckled before he hung up.

Ang put the bowl of popcorn down on her sister's bed and crossed her arms. Ash gave me a wide-eyed look.

"What?" I asked.

"Don't we hate him?" Ang replied.

"If this can take my mind off this past weekend, I don't care," I said, walking over to my closet.

When Kadeem knocked on our door, I had just finished doing my makeup. Ash opened the door, and a smirk appeared on his proud mouth when he saw me. I gave a small smile before walking over to put on my jacket.

"I love the dress," he said.

"Thanks," I replied, casually.

"Alright, let's get out of here," Ang piped in, and we all followed her out the door.

That night, we bar hopped and danced. It was just what I needed to not think about everything that happened back in New York. When we got back to our dorm building, Kadeem and I wandered behind the twins. He had held up his end of the bargain and paid for all my food and drinks, in return, I had a good time. In a swift move, as we got to his door, he pulled me in for a kiss. It was a type of kiss that made you forget how to walk. He held me upward as I kissed him back. I didn't make it back to my room that night.

The next morning, I got back to the dorm room early, but not early enough for Ash. She sat at the kitchen table in her fluffy white robe and her hair up. I froze when I saw her, but she continued to sip her coffee.

"Good morning, bestie." I smiled.

"Oh, don't start. All I have to say is what the hell," she hissed the words in between sips.

"I know, it's just that it's him, and he's always been my… kryptonite," I reasoned..

"This is not fast food, Rachel. This is a man. A man who has fucked up royally in the past."

"I know," I sighed.

"So are you two back together?" Ash asked right before my phone pinged.

I looked down to see a text from Kadeem. I raised a brow at it before I tapped on the screen, prompting Ash to stand up and look at my texts over my shoulder.

Kadeem White: Hey, I miss you already. Let's get breakfast before you have class this afternoon.

"What did you do to him?" Ash asked, and I wagged my eyebrows at her, a slight smirk gathering at my lips.

Rachel Smith: Sure. Meet me in an hour.

We decided to eat at a diner a few miles away. Kadeem's car wasn't on campus, but mine was, so I offered to drive. It had been some days since I had driven my SUV, and Dad had always said to make sure I run it at least every couple weeks. When we got to the car, Kadeem noticed a puddle, took the opportunity to examine it,and explained that brake fluid was leaking. We drove to the nearest mechanic shop. Kadeem took the liberty of speaking to the mechanic, and I happily laid back and looked around since I didn't know a thing about cars.

When we got outside, I called Dad and he said he would transfer over the money I needed to fix it—over five hundred dollars. After that, Kadeem and I walked around and got coffee while we waited. The mechanic called us back soon after and said my car would be ready soon.

Kadeem firmly held my hand as we walked into the shop. He and the guy at the front desk spoke about my car, and I zoned out again until it was time for me to pay. The two walked further into the building as they continued to discuss cars in a capacity that was enough to nauseate me. I turned to the employee, who was giving me a very unprofessional once over, and walked up to the cash register.

"How much do I owe you guys?" I sighed as I purposely showed my disinterest in him.

"It's… Uh…. It's already paid, miss." He looked at the computer screen in front of him with a confused squint.

"Excuse me?" I asked after a moment.

"It's confusing. It says here that there was one deposit and then there is an even… larger deposit here after. It's paid already," he speculated as his eyes danced between me and the screen. He seemed to be watching to see if I was going to make any sudden movements.

"Who were the payments made by?" I asked.

"By some—" the man began, but then he was cut off by Kadeem, who put a warm arm around me.

"By me, babe," Kadeem exclaimed with a kiss to a temple, "I had to make sure you were all straight. Anything for you."

I wanted to further investigate where he got the money to afford that especially for a more expensive SUV, but I did appreciate the effort. It just made me feel a little strange. Before I could press further, he whisked me to my SUV and made sure I was seated comfortably in my driver's seat. There was something that was really questionable about his movements, but I couldn't pinpoint it. There was too much going on. I waited for him to run over and sit in the passenger's seat next to me, but he didn't.

"Come on, Deem, get in the car," I said.

"No, that's alright. I have to get some stuff done on this side of the city," he said.

"So, I'll drive you. It's the least I could do."

"No, thank you. You should go back to campus for class," he said coldly before walking out of the garage.

I looked around at the two other men in the shop, but they averted their gazes. I slowly drove off. I had a bad feeling in my stomach as I parked in the campus parking lot and walked over to my dorm building. I wasn't sure why. Nothing was wrong, from what I could see, at least. When I got into my dorm suite, I saw Ash and Ang sitting down. Ang gave me a concerned frown, and it was almost validating to know someone else thought something was wrong too.

"Hey guys, what's up?" I asked after a moment of silence.

"Rachel, you should sit down," Ang insisted, and the use of my full name along with her tone told me it was serious.

I took a seat at the kitchen table and set my bag down in the vacant seat. I looked over at Ash, but her face was not reassuring. The thumbs on her folded hands danced with each other.

"What is it?" I prodded.

"I know it's finals and things aren't the best at home right now. Maybe we should wait until Friday when finals are over," Ash said, unsure.

"Okay, well I'm not going to wait for four days," I said.

"Don't freak out, but I think Kadeem is seeing Taylor again," Ang spoke softly.

I scoffed and rolled my eyes. The twins looked at each other with an expression only sisters would understand before turning back to me. They must've thought they saw something that they really didn't. I mean, I just saw the man.

"I was just with Kadeem twenty minutes ago. He paid for my car to get fixed," I told them, gesturing widely as if my car was right there to prove it.

"Well, we just saw him and Taylor together ten minutes ago. They were grabbing coffee at Martha's," Ash answered.

Martha's was a cafe that was just a couple blocks away from the mechanic. I had gone there multiple times, even with Kadeem. I wanted things to just be a coincidence. That's all I wanted, and while it wasn't for the best reasons—being tired of things not working out with guys and not wanting everyone to be right about him—at that moment, I didn't really care. I really wanted my person to be him, mainly for my sanity.

"It's probably nothing, guys. He just *paid* the bill for my car to get fixed. I think he's trying to be more serious this time," I said.

"Look, I don't want to get involved in other people's relationships," Ang started.

"Then don't," I snapped before I really thought about what I was saying.

Ang tilted her head over to Ash with an exasperated sigh before she picked up her mini backpack. She started to make her way to the door.

"Ash, the patience department is your thing. I have a date tonight, anyway," she said.

"With Ethan?" Ash asked with a raised eyebrow.

"Yeah. I don't know how it happened, but I'm actually not nauseated by his face." Ang shrugged.

"Have fun," I offered.

"Thanks, and don't be stupid, babe," Ang said, pointing tiredly at me before she walked out the door.

Chapter 6

Josh

Against my brother's wishes, I decided to go back home to Soteria. Being in the apartment with Noah and Nicole was nice, but they were very much still in their honeymoon phase, and, despite their efforts, I felt like a third wheel. One of Noah's drivers drove me up, which meant I had two hours with someone who was not going to try to speak to me if I did not want to.

After about an hour of silent driving and watching the buildings give way to the mountains and trees, I finally dug my phone out of my bag. I had a recent missed call from my friend Nina. I put the partition up and tapped on my screen to call her back.

"Hey stranger, how's the city?" Her voice answered.

"Neens, how are you? And the city was okay. Some family drama, but it is what it is," I said.

"Is everyone okay?

"Not right now, but I think it'll work out."

"What *great* details. Anyway, I wanted to know if you were coming home today. I went to see my grandparents this morning, so I'm less than an hour away," she said.

Nina was my best friend, and we usually would tell each other everything. Normally, I didn't have much to spill, but with everything that happened with my family, there had been some changes. I would have loved to share it with her, but it seemed like it was best to not. In this world, it seemed like the less you knew, the better. I didn't ask to know all that I did, but also, I didn't ask more than what was offered. I guess carrying burdens was the birthright of any son of Carter Crawford.

"Yeah, I should be home in an hour," I said.

"Cool, I'll see you in a little bit. I'll bring pizza," she sang before hanging up.

I walked inside the house and started straight for the stairs when I noticed something in the corner of my eye. I backed up slowly to find my brother sitting on the couch with his laptop. I stood there for a moment waiting for him to notice me, but his headphones kept him wrapped in his little bubble.

"Hi Jason," I said, grabbing a pillow on a nearby chair and throwing it in his direction.

He looked up, clearly startled, and smiled casually. He straightened his glasses and placed his headphones on the couch he was sitting on. His books on the coffee table told he had been here for a while.

"Hey, what's up?" Jason asked.

"I'm alright. When did you get here?" I asked, a little thrown off by the fact that he didn't say why he was in, what was mainly, my house.

"I had my last in-person final yesterday. The last one is online tomorrow, so I figured I would come by and see you before I get busy with Christmas. You should come to Jersey with me," he said, getting up to give me a fist bump.

"I'm the subject of a manhunt, remember?" I asked dryly.

"We haven't heard from Tracey in months. You should spend your time the way you want to," Jason said.

The truth was, I was not entirely sure I wanted to spend my time there anyway. Did I really want to spend time with the lady, who, I was pretty sure, knew I was alive this whole time and the guy I used to call dad, who also seemed to know something was amiss and didn't do much? I mean, I don't know about you, but the answer seems to be quite clear. I was saved from having to think of a response that would not disappoint him, when the bell rang. I set my bag down and walked over to the door. In the peephole, I saw Nina with a large bag on her shoulder and a big pizza box. I opened the door.

"Long time, no see," I said as I took the box from her.

"It's been forever," she said with a smile.

"How was the drive from Albany?" I set the box on the kitchen island.

"It was quick. I listened to an episode of a gaming podcast, and, before I knew it, I was here. Hug me," she gushed, pulling me into a hug.

I complied, wrapping my arms around her. It had been so long since the last time we had seen each other in person. I always video-chatted with Nina when we gamed, but it had to be a little over six months since we'd hung out in person. The only time before that was the first time we met. I guess we weren't the typical set of best friends. For about ten years, I had thought Nina would be my person, in a romantic sense, but she wasn't. I felt nothing, and I knew it hurt her a lot. I was just glad we were able to remain friends. I really didn't have anyone else, especially then.

"Someone else is here?" Nina asked, slowly pulling away from me.

"Don't let me interrupt the reunion y'all have going on over there." Jason chuckled from the living room.

"Jason, this is my friend Nina. Nina, this is my brother Jason," I introduced the two.

Jason slowly slid off his glasses as he approached Nina, and I could already tell from his expression what he was thinking. His eyes cut to mine for a split second, and I returned the question in his eyes with a slight raise of my shoulder. He shook her one hand with two of his and let his hands linger for a moment before realizing he held it for too long and letting them go.

"Nina Perez. Nice to meet you, Jason," she greeted warmly.

"It's nice to meet you, Nina. I've heard great things. Josh, you didn't tell me you have such gorgeous friends," he said in a velvety voice that made me look up at the ceiling for a second to keep myself from vomiting.

I was fully aware that, objectively, Nina was beautiful. She had this heart shaped face with these striking cheekbones and some nice lips too. At some point, I wanted to be in love with her. I really tried, but I just wasn't.

"You're too kind." Nina laughed lightly, a blush darkening her cheeks.

Clearing my throat to interrupt, I said, "Alright, do you want to set the game up? I'm going to run into the shower real quick."

"Yeah, I'll go do that. I'll bring the pizza up too," she said before giving Jason a smile and walking upstairs.

When I looked over to Jason, he was already staring at me with a suggestive smirk. I laughed and shook my head.

"What?" I asked.

"Nina is a fucking smoke show," he whistled.

"She is very pretty, yes," I agreed, walking over to grab my duffle bag.

"Are you going to make a move, or should I?"

"That ship has sailed. We're just friends. I told you about that."

"Can I?"

"I thought you were still in love with our favorite married woman," I deadpanned.

"That doesn't mean I don't have needs, and I haven't seen anyone this past year. I'm not you," he scoffed.

"What's that supposed to mean?" I laughed.

"You're living the life of a seminarian," he said.

"Oh, relax. I am not. I told you about what happened with Nina. Just because I didn't sleep with her doesn't mean nothing happened at all. You didn't sleep with Nicole," I reminded him quietly.

"Nicole and I were friends in the beginning."

"Great, and Nina is my friend. I'm not going to let sex make things complicated. I rather wait until I find whoever is worth making things complicated with."

"You're so strange," Jason huffed.

"And your rebound phase post-Nicole has made you gross." I shook my head, escaping upstairs.

Around four-thirty the next morning, I realized that Nina and I had both fallen asleep on my bed, but I was too tired to do anything about it. I threw the blanket over her and fell back asleep. The next time, I woke up to the sun coming through my blinds. I looked over to see that Nina was not there. I brushed my teeth and went downstairs to find where she had gone. I found her in the kitchen, making waffles, with Jason sitting down at the table, mesmerized by the sight of her.

"Good morning," I yawned.

"Morning, sleepyhead," Nina beamed.

"What's all of this?" I asked.

"You made me breakfast last time I stayed, so I figured I would return the favor. Jason kept me company," she said.

"I'm sure he did," I said dryly.

"I have my final in an hour, so I wasn't going to pass up a good meal." Jason gave an honest shrug.

"What's your major?" Nina asked, genuinely curious.

"Pre-law," Jason said.

"Ah, a future lawyer. When do you graduate?"

"Next semester will be my last. I'll be done early. My four year, eight season show was cut down to two years and four seasons," Jason joked proudly.

"Ha, I get it, but that's impressive! I know Josh said you were younger than us, and you're finishing up college already? Congratulations," Nina said, and I could tell by the slight frown decorating his face that Jason didn't like being referred to as *young*.

My phone rang in my pocket, and I slid it out to look at the screen. Rachel's name showed across the screen, so I answered.

"Hey Rachel," I said.

"Hey Joshy, do you have a minute?" Rachel's voice answered from the other side of the phone.

"*Josh* has a minute," I challenged.

"Fine, *Josh*. I need your help with something."

"And what is that?"

"Do you think you can hack into someone's phone for me?"

"Possibly, depending on how they store the stuff on their phone. Why?"

"Promise you won't tell your brother and my sister?"

I paused for a moment. "Yeah, I promise."

"I just feel like he's up to something. I need to find out. I don't have the mental space to wonder right now. I could be completely overthinking everything, but what if I'm not? Sometimes it's the "what if" that ruins everything that's right in front of you."

"He, as in Kadeem, I'm assuming?" I disappeared into the office to speak out of ear range. Jason and Nina had stopped speaking and seemed curious.

"Yeah. Something's wrong. He said he paid for my car to be fixed, but honestly, I don't think he did," she said.

"Um, I'm a little confused, but I can help. Give me all the information you have on him and the name of the mechanic shop," I said, pulling out my laptop.

Chapter 7

Josh

I felt someone's presence in my room, and I turned around to see Nina standing in my doorway. She gave me a hesitant smile as she moved further into the room. I closed down my window. I trusted Nina, but I didn't want her to be aware that I wasn't sharing with her. It was better this way.

"Hey, what are you up to?" she asked.

"Nothing much," I said, casually.

She furrowed her eyebrows and crossed her arms. "Why don't you speak to me anymore?"

I chuckled and stood up to face her.

"What do you mean? I speak to you all the time."

"No, you don't really speak to me. You…"

"What?"

"Nothing. Your phone is lighting up. Looks like Rachel is calling you *again*... Jason wants to go out for ice cream. Do you want to come with?" Nina asked, the disappointment evident in her voice.

I really did not want to get ice cream in the middle of the winter. I wasn't sure why my brother wanted to eat something cold when the temperatures were so low. I hesitated only because there seemed to be more hanging on how I decided to answer.

"Let us know. We're leaving in like twenty minutes," she sighed, walking out the room.

The phone had stopped ringing, so I called Rachel back. When the call picked up, background noise answered first. It usually sounded like that when she called while driving.

"Hey," she said.

"Hi, uh, I have access to some of this guy's stuff on his cloud, but not all. He uses some heavily encrypted apps."

She sighed heavily, and I immediately felt like I had failed her. I finally was able to get into some of his text messages, but I wasn't sure how much I was going to be able to see. There was a slow loading screen before I was able to see a folder with some names. I saw "Rachel Smith", "Mom", "Dad", someone named "Zeke", and a few other names that did not ring any bells. My eyes fell on a folder that was titled "Taylor Morris". At first, I skipped it, but then I went back to it. It had the largest amount of bytes and the name kept ringing a bell.

"Do you know a Taylor Morris?" I asked.

"*Do I know her?* She's the bane of my fucking existence," she said, exasperated.

"Interesting. Is this the girl that you told me you wanted to throw down the stairs a few months ago?"

"The one and only. What about her?" There was something so unsettling in her voice, like she would contemplate actually doing something like that. What was even more unsettling was that I found humor in the thought.

"She just has a really big folder, but I can't access anything inside it. It could be old stuff, though," I said, trying to ease her nerves. It must've been hard to trust the guy after everything that happened that last spring.

Things got quieter on her side of the phone, and it sounded like she had parked. We had been on the phone so many times that I didn't have to ask anymore. I already knew. Now her car was off, and she was sitting in her car on the phone, protected from the cold. She still had not said anything.

"Rachel?"

"Yes, Joshua?" She must've been upset because she only said my full name like that when she was really frustrated or trying not to cry. I'd never actually heard or seen her cry, but I had heard her choke and push back her emotions.

"If I may, why are you stressing out over some loser? There are other guys," I murmured, treading lightly.

"You don't understand," she groaned, and she was right, I didn't.

***

Yup, I was a complete and utter fool, an imbecile, a simpleton, a moron. I was stupid. I was stupid to think that this could be a possibility. Why did I think that Rachel would want me to take her to prom? It was a very stupid idea, but over the weeks that I'd known her, she had confided to me about her fears of going alone. Then, I got the idea that maybe I could go with her. I told you, it was a stupid idea, but it was my idea, and when I set my mind to something, I would get really down when they didn't work out.

As she spoke to me on the phone, I tried to force my voice to sound as unphased as possible. I would have to pull a Noah. He cared, but he barely showed that he did and it seemed like it worked for him.

"Isn't that great? He asked me! He asked me to be his date to prom," Rachel squealed on the phone.

"That's great! I'm happy for you. So everything you did worked, I guess," I said through gritted teeth.

"Yeah, I guess. I'm so excited! I have my dress, but I have so much stuff to still shop for," Rachel continued.

"Well, Kadeem is a lucky guy."

"I have to call the twins! Bye Josh. Thanks for always listening to me go on about this. Love you, bye!"

I felt my shoulders fall before I threw my phone across my room. I had a hard time processing it all. I just knew that I was upset, but I shouldn't be. I lost.

Later that day, I heard someone downstairs. Maybe everyone decided to come up for the weekend. I walked downstairs and saw Noah standing there by himself. No one else was around.

"Sorry, expecting someone else?" he asked dryly.

"Oh, I was just hoping you brought the gang," I said, trying not to sound disappointed.

"No," he sighed.

"What's wrong?" I asked, seeing how down and deflated he seemed. I could

relate.

"I'm getting a divorce," Noah said, and it was the first time his voice revealed

what he was truly feeling, sad.

"I forgot about that. I'm sorry, man. I know you love her," I said, hugging him.

"What's all this?" He changed the subject.

"I think we both need a hug right now," I said.

Noah slowly pulled away and raised an eyebrow in question. I rubbed at my eyes, trying to make whatever the hell they thought they were going to do to stop immediately.

***

I walked downstairs to join Jason and Nina on their quest for hypothermia when I immediately came to a stop by the sight of Eliza standing in the foyer. She was standing next to her white suitcase, large sunglasses on top of her head, even though it wasn't sunny. She gave me a half smile.

"Hey pretty boy, I'm going to be here for a couple weeks," she said dryly.

"Why?" I asked, slowly walking toward her.

"Because my parents are going away without me for the holidays. Pretty fucking rude if you ask me." She sighed, seeming bored with it all.

"They were going to leave you in the house alone for Christmas? Yikes, I'm sorry," I said.

"I'm not surprised. Anyway, where are you off to?"

"I'm going to join Jason and Nina for ice cream. You want to come? It's cold as ice out, but I guess no one cares about that."

"Yeah, sure. Who's Nina?"

"My friend," I said.

"Ooh, what kind of friend?" Eliza's left eyebrow went up from behind her sunglasses.

"Why is it that a guy and girl can't be platonic?"

"They can… I would know," Eliza mumbled under her breath.

We sat in the ice cream parlor, eating our concoctions in a booth that was clearly too small for four average sized adults, but somehow we made it work. I sat next to Eliza, across from Nina and Jason.

"What the hell are you eating, Westbrook?" Eliza scrunched her nose at the large cup of peanut butter and mint ice cream mixture Jason had in front of him.

"It's not as bad as it looks," he answered with his mouth full.

"It makes sense you would eat something so disgusting," Eliza hissed.

"I may be *disgusting*, but at least my parents will still want to be around me after it," he retorted, though I could tell he regretted saying it the moment it came out his mouth.

"Dude," I exhaled.

Jason grimaced and peered back up at Eliza. She just stared at him blankly.

"That was really out of line. I'm sorry," Jason said, his eyes wide.

Eliza looked over at Nina and then out the window. She probably wanted to say so much but couldn't, not in front of Nina. There was such a sad look in her eyes that it made me feel this overbearing feeling of empathy. I think Jason felt it too. A year ago, things would have been a lot different if Eliza hadn't saved his life. I wasn't there for it, but Noah had told me. So had Rachel. Eliza saved their lives the night I met everyone. If she hadn't, someone could have died.

"I'm really sorry, Eliza," Jason repeated after a moment of silence.

"Just *stop*," Eliza whispered, her voice sticking on the last word. He did.

Chapter 8

Rachel

I packed my suitcase for the trip home as I waited for Kadeem to show up. We weren't going to see each other for about three weeks. He and his family were going away for Christmas, and after that, he mentioned that he would have to be back on campus for a meeting. I didn't want to come off as the clingy type, so my only request was that I would get to spend time with him on my last night in Philly for several weeks.

Since the mechanic shop, I had only seen Kadeem once, and it was to study together. Finals had just ended, and it was a busy time for both of us. I still had lots of questions running through my mind about what the twins had mentioned before. I wanted to ask questions, but I just couldn't. I promised myself that I would ask that night. I needed to know. It was starting to stress me out.

My dorm suite was pretty quiet. The twins had already headed back home, just like a lot of other students who lived in the building. I usually savored the rare quiet moments in the building, but now, all I wanted was some noise to fill up the weird vibe that I couldn't shake. I checked my phone for any texts, and I only had one from Josh.

Annoying Ass: Got a new high score on Glitcher. We still on for a rematch tomorrow?

Me: Be prepared to lose.

Annoying Ass: Oh it's like that?

Me: When do you not lose in my presence?

Annoying Ass: Years off my life? Possibly. Games? No.

Me: Keep lying to yourself, Joshy.

Annoying Ass: Besides being delusional, what are you up to?

I was about to text a response when I heard a knock on my door. I threw my phone over to my bed and looked through the peephole. There Kadeem stood with his coat in his hand and a white shirt pulled over his muscles. I stood up on my toes so he could give me a kiss like he had been doing the past couple days, but instead, he just cleared his throat. My stomach immediately formed knots.

"What's wrong with you?" I asked.

"Nothing. I'm just coming down with something," he said before clearing his throat.

"Oh, ok," I said.

"What are you up to?"

"Just packing. Are you ready for your trip?"

"Yeah, I better be. I'm meeting my parents at the airport in the morning."

There was something that seemed so off about him. I couldn't put my finger on it, though. I took a step near him again, but he took a step away.

"You sure you're okay?" I finally asked, feeling like I already knew the answer.

"Yeah, I'm fine," he said.

"Are we good?"

"Why do you ask?" He shifted his weight, like he was uncomfortable.

"Because you're usually all over me. You're not going to see me for three weeks and you don't want to come near me… Are you seeing Taylor again?" I asked, unable to face him as I did. Maybe I already knew the answer.

"Rachel, listen," he began.

"You are. Get out. I can't look at you!" I stepped back, opening the door.

"I can explain." He put his hand out, but I shifted away.

"It's always her. I'm not doing this again. Don't even look at me next semester. Now, get out," I demanded.

"I'm sorry, Rachel. It's not you. You're beautiful, but Taylor and I have a connection."

"Do me a favor? Don't give me that pity speech, okay? We've been there and done that before. That's also bullshit. She has the personality of a cactus, but she is your definition of beautiful, and I'm not," I said.

"Now Rachel, let's keep it classy," he said in the most patronizing tone, and I wanted to slap him for it, but I didn't.

"Tell me that's not it." I crossed my arms.

"I don't know. I'm sorry you feel this way. Merry Christmas," he sighed awkwardly as he started walking to the door.

"Just answer me one more question. Did you pay for my car or not?" I blinked back tears.

He looked down like he was deep in thought for a moment before he looked at me, sympathy softening his eyes.

"No, I didn't," he answered.

"Then who did?"

"I don't know. They said if I… I don't know who they are, Rachel. They said nothing bad would happen, and they would make sure I got a B plus in chemistry so I could stay in sports," he said.

"Who the fuck? That sounds so shady, Kadeem. There are people who are crazy out there and want to kill people. You just let some random people do something to my car? You really could give less of a shit about my existence." I laughed in anger.

He raised his hands in defense. "I didn't think about it that way."

"Get out because besides being selfish, you're also an idiot." I pointed to the door.

He started to walk out, but opened the door again right before it closed. I groaned this time because, unfortunately, the hell of hearing this thought process was not over.

"For what it's worth, I always thought you were super funny and a great person. I mean that. I always really liked that about you," he said, then closed the door behind him when he realized that I was not going to respond.

It was at that moment I came to the conclusion that if I looked like Taylor—light skinned and light eyes, we wouldn't be having this conversation. Who I was, was not enough. I walked to my window and watched him saunter off. Guess who he held hands with as he walked down the street? Taylor Morris. Taylor Morris with her beige colored skin and long curls that bounced down her back. Taylor Morris, the absolute opposite of me.

I threw the rest of the things I wanted to bring over break in my suitcase and started driving. I didn't head back home. That was the last place I wanted to be. Instead of going east, I went north, and I didn't stop until I got to a rest stop about two hours later. I looked at my phone to see where I was and found I had driven all the way to upstate New York. Scrolling through notifications, I found that no one had called me. I wished Nicole had called. She probably would've used some smart vocabulary to talk about how much of an idiot Kadeem was just to make me laugh. Although, part of me wondered if she even understood what it was like for me. Nicole was by no means someone who would be considered light, but she was lighter than me. She was light enough. Everyone thought she was beautiful and revered her like she was a princess. I didn't get looked at like that. Noah never made her feel uncomfortable about her hair or skin tone. She got lucky, I guess, but I did wonder, at times, if her luck made her blind to what others' misfortunes were.

I decided on Soteria. When I got there, I rang the bell. It was getting late. I was expecting to see Caesar or maybe Josh answer the door, but instead, a girl with long brown hair and strong cheekbones answered the door. She seemed familiar, but I couldn't pinpoint who she was. With a wry smile, she opened the door wider for me to come in.

"Who are you?" I asked, not thinking about manners.

"I'm Nina, and you're Rachel, right? I recognize your voice," she said in a tone that sounded like it was trying its best to sound warm but failed.

"Hey, Nina. Nice to meet you," I said as it finally clicked that I knew her because of Josh.

"Who is it, Neens?" Josh's smooth voice filled the air as he walked down the stairs.

Josh had on his gaming headset and a black shirt to match his black sweatpants. His bright eyes squinted in question. All I could do was stare back. He pulled the headset off his ears and rested it on his neck. He took a few more steps until he was standing near myself and Nina. She glanced back and forth between us.

"Nina, can you give us a minute?" He asked, not taking his eyes off me.

"Yeah." She hesitated before walking upstairs.

When she was gone, he took another step near me and put his hands in his pockets. It was silent for another moment until I spoke. He was always patient in that way— never pushing me to say things until I wanted to.

"Kadeem and I ended things… whatever it was," I said.

"I'm sorry," he said.

"No, you're not."

"I am. I don't like him, but I know you did," Josh exhaled.

"I don't know why I came here. I just didn't want to go back home, especially after what happened last time I was there." I ran a hand over my face.

"You know you're always welcomed here," he said.

"Thanks." I nodded.

"Yeah, now I can see your face when I annihilate your ass at *Glitcher*." He smirked.

I tried to chuckle, but instead, my focus rested on not crying. I tried my best not to do that in front of people. I ran my hands over my jeans before putting them in my back pockets.

"He's an idiot. If he can't see that he's losing the best thing that will ever happen to him, then he's an idiot," Josh said.

"I think I could have almost died. Maybe? I don't know."

He stepped forward. "What happened?"

"He said he didn't pay for my car to get fixed but promised someone he would bring my car to the mechanic shop in exchange for a good grade in chemistry," I said.

Josh's whole demeanor changed as he took his headphones off and threw it on the couch when he got close enough from beginning to pace.

"Scratch that, he's an asshat. Does he know how stupid that is? Who asked him to do that? That's some weird Tracey shit," he rambled.

"I don't know. He didn't say who it was, but I wouldn't be surprised if it was her." I turned away, sinking into the recliner.

He scratched the back of his head. "Something must've gone wrong on Tracey's end because your car is fine."

"The man at the shop did say there were two deposits put down," I said with a shrug.

Josh stared at the fireplace in silence. There were so many emotions going on in his eyes, but the most recognizable one was anger.

"We'll figure this out after the holidays, but what I'm most happy about is that you're okay," he said.

He didn't say he told me so. He simply was happy that I was safe. In a very out of character moment, I gave him a hug, and he hugged me back.

Chapter 9

Rachel

Christmas was never not a big deal at the Smith residence. Despite the insane work schedules of both of my parents, they always made every Christmas amazing. Every year, I looked forward to it, even after things had changed during the trial with Noah back in high school. This year was different, though. I would be home with my parents, and they even agreed to let Nicole spend the day there so we could all be together as a family, yet something was obviously off.

I wrapped my presents last minute on Christmas Eve. Nicole and I would usually wrap our presents together, but of course, we didn't this time. I offered the idea of doing so over a video call, but she didn't want to. I'd barely heard from Nicole in the few weeks following the incident. When she had decided that anxiety with heights that rivaled Mount Everest was a substantial punishment for my sins, she finally answered a few of my texts and would respond a couple times a day so I would at least know she was alive. It wasn't enough, but I was happy to hear from her. I missed her. I was beyond sorry, and I was worried that she was not doing well handling being closed out by Mom and Dad, The Table, *and* still going to school. I would check in with Noah to make sure she wasn't crumbling, but he was brief in his responses. I don't think it was purposeful. He had a crap ton of things on his plate too, which made me feel even worse about adding this situation onto it.

I was never one to buckle under stress. I would dust off my shoulders and just power through. It's what I did. I did it because there was a point in time when Nicole couldn't and I had to do it for her. It was a weird feeling like there was a weight on my chest every morning. It would take much longer to get up in the mornings, the days leading up to Christmas. Everything seemed to take up more energy. I wondered if that's how Nicole felt everyday for years, or if she still had moments like that now. She never spoke about how everything affected her mentally, but if it was anything like how I felt that holiday season, then it would make sense.

By the time Christmas day came along, I was almost crawling out of bed. I took a long shower and made a huge mug of coffee to give me some strength because I had used all of what I already had to get up and look pretty. I plastered on a smile for Mom and Dad, willing my heart to not race as we waited for Nicole to show up for breakfast and gifts.

Soon enough, the bell rang, and Dad beat me to the door. An awkward silence followed his opening of the door. He and Nicole just stared at each other for a moment.

"Hey Dad," she finally said.

"How are you?" Dad asked, painfully formal.

"Good, glad to be done with this semester. It was a tough one." Her words seemed so rehearsed.

"Hey baby," Mom smiled, walking up and pulling her in for a hug.

"Hi, Mom, how are you?" Nicole asked, her voice strained.

"I'm alright," Mom answered softly with a touch of concern.

Nicole put her tote of presents down and looked over at me. I smiled, and she did too, except hers was obviously ingenuine. It was almost like her eyes were glossed over, and she was just… I don't know, it was like she was a robot. Nicole was always poised and calculated, but this time, she almost seemed dead.

"Hey Rachel," she hesitated, pulling me in for a loose hug. Not Rach, not Chelly, but Rachel. I almost asked her to start over.

"Hey Coco," I sighed.

She pulled away quickly, her shoulders lowering like she was able to breathe again. I watched her grab the handle of her tote and bring it over to the tree. She didn't take out the presents like I expected her to, but just placed the bag next to the tree and stared at it for a long uncomfortable moment before turning to look at us. I think Dad noticed something was wrong, but he didn't say anything and just kept his gaze focused on his shoes. Mom made eye contact with me with a frown that I couldn't read the meaning behind. *Was that accusatory or just observant?* I wasn't sure.

"Well, I don't want to delay opening gifts any longer, so let's get to it," Mom said, trying her best.

"Same," I said.

I skipped toward the tree to lighten the mood and started handing boxes to everyone. Then Mom started handing out presents and Dad followed. Nicole grabbed her bag and handed out her gifts too. I opened her gift first —it was a new dance bag with my name stitched on the suede material. I pulled her in for a hug. The gift was beautiful, but, really, I just missed her. She slowly wrapped her arms loosely around me and hugged me back.

"I'm glad you like it," she said softly.

"I'm just glad you're here, Coco."

"Yeah," she agreed shakily.

I pulled away to look her in the eyes. Something was wrong, and *yeah I know*, everything was wrong already, but there was something more there. I stared at her for a moment and then glanced around, realizing that Dad hadn't gotten her a gift. He tactfully kept his eyes on Mom. I had never been so disappointed in him, not until that moment. It wasn't an oversight or money being tight—it was on purpose. He did it to make a statement that he hadn't forgiven what happened.

That evening at dinner, we all ate in purposeful silence. I wanted to ease the tension in the air by speaking, but just couldn't get myself to say anything. It was like the weight of what had happened before kept my mouth shut. I finally locked eyes with Nicole, and she huffed silently. She finally turned to Mom and spoke.

"So, Mom, how's the book club going?"

Mom looked up, almost in shock that Nicole had dared to break the ice. She was silent for a moment as if she did not know what to say. She cleared her throat.

"It's going well. We just finished up a holiday novel earlier this week. We'll probably do another mystery next month. Karen hasn't told us what book she's chosen yet," Mom said.

"I need to get back to my normal reading schedule. Send me the book the club decides to read. I might pick it up too so we can discuss," Nicole offered, and I could tell she was really trying to make some sort of truce.

"I definitely will! You should read the romance we read last month. I loved it," Mom said, completely getting distracted by the conversation.

"Speaking of romance, how's Noah doing?" Dad asked, and I rolled my eyes at his choice of transition. Totally subtle.

Nicole paused for a moment and took a few extra long seconds to chew her food as she thought of a way to answer his question. She knew she had to play her cards just right. Mom would be easy to win back, but Dad, he would be a different story.

"He's doing well. He's spending Christmas with Josh upstate. I'll be heading up there tonight." Nicole smiled.

"Well, please give everyone my regards," Dad said, and it was clear that's all he had to say for the moment. Dad always loved chatting with his eldest and nerdiest daughter, so it was weird hearing him only having two sentences to say. I prayed for things to go back to normal soon. I had to remind myself that this was a huge improvement from what happened a month ago. With time, things would get better. In a few months time, we would all be laughing about this, right? At least, that's what I told myself as I watched Nicole sadly observe her plate. All we needed was more time.

"So, how long?" Mom asked.

"What do you mean?" Nicole asked.

"How long have you two been married?" Mom asked as she glanced over to see Dad's pained expression.

"It'll be a year in a few days," Nicole softly recalled.

It was crazy to think about, really. Our lives had changed so much over the course of that year. If someone would have walked up to me and told me that I would know the things I knew in that moment, I probably would've asked what they were smoking. Dad frowned and nodded when he realized that he really had not known about such a huge part about Nicole's life for so long. Nicole turned her plate again. It wasn't fair. She didn't want it to be this way, but if they knew, it could be dangerous.

"I'm glad you found your person," Mom said softly, and Nicole looked over at her with a sad, sure smile. There were so many things I pitied her for in that moment, but her love life was not one of them. In fact, at times, I was pretty jealous. When all else failed, Noah loved her ferociously, and she would always have that.

Nicole and I sat by the fire pit on the patio after dinner. It was quiet at first, but I was happy that she wanted to be around me at all. I watched as the light of the fire flickered around her face. She wrapped her blanket around herself tighter before she looked over at me.

"How was this semester for you?" She asked, her voice soothing.

"It was good, just busy," I replied.

"It's an adjustment, especially with you being on the dance team, but I know you got this," she said.

"Thanks."

"How's Kadeem?" she asked after a few beats.

"Being a piece of garbage on an island somewhere… Completely polluting it," I sneered.

She didn't say anything. She just continued to watch the fire.

"I hate myself for even speaking to him again," I added.

"I try not to judge because we all know Noah is not perfect, but why him?" Nicole asked. She had a point —Noah was very much not perfect, but in a different sense. Yes, I know. *What? You're not taking the opportunity to insult your brother-in-law?* I am, by no means, the biggest fan of Noah Crawford. That being said, I realize that he is a decent partner to my sister and would never embarrass her like Kadeem had done to me.

"I don't know," I answered honestly because the truth was, I really didn't know. I just wanted him to want me back as much as I wanted him. At least, that's what I used to want. What I wanted at that point was for him to diligently play in traffic.

"As someone who has married *GQ* meets the *Godfather* personified, I—" she began, but I had to stop her.

"Excuse me?" I screamed.

"It's true! Look at him." She chuckled.

"I'm literally screaming." I sat up straighter.

"Ha, I think between you and Noah, I've gotten a little meaner." She tried to frown but kept laughing.

"Amazing." I smiled.

"But seriously, life can be hard, but you need someone who is going to cherish you; someone who will go the extra mile for you. I know I can't be mad at you for going back to the guy because I also went back to the guy. But, not this guy. Please, not this one," Nicole begged.

"Guys don't worship the ground I walk like they do for you," I said.

"Yes, they do," she shook her head, her eyebrows drawn together.

"No, they don't. I'm the funny one. You're the one they fall in love with," I said confidently. I even had evidence to back up my claims.

I lost count of how many guys had taken me on dates or became my friend because I was considered the knockoff version of my sister. Everyone always spoke about her. She would come up in conversations, even when the topic was about me, people would ask what my sister thought. I loved and completely revered my sister, but it was a little too much at times.

"Rachel, we are completely different people who bring different things to the table. Both of those things are of value," she said, using her big sister voice like she did at times that rivaled a teacher's lecture.

I sighed and shook my head. I didn't want to have this conversation again. It was hard for the person who benefited from the situation to understand what the person who didn't was going through. Society, unfortunately, knew a lot about that.

"I have to start driving up. I'm going to say bye to Mom and Dad," she said.

"Why aren't you spending the night and leaving in the morning?"

"Mom, Dad, and I are *not* there yet. I think we'll get there though. Noah and I were talking, and we agreed that, after graduation, we would have a real ceremony with them involved. It would make them feel as if they didn't miss out on that part. We have a couple years to worry about that, though," she said, her voice both sad and hopeful. I hugged my sister goodbye, and she went inside, leaving me in front of the flames.

After Nicole left, I went up to my room and started to organize my gifts. The day had gone somewhat well, but something in my gut made me feel so unsettled. I called Ash to see what she was up to. She didn't answer. Almost instantly, I realized I had a text from her.

Ashlyn Dumas: Hey, SOS. Would really help if you came over!!

Rachel Smith: Hey Ash. Just saw this. What's up?

I waited for about fifteen minutes, but there was no answer. There was something weird about her text. Ash never used so much punctuation–maybe something was up. I threw some clothes in a bag and started to walk downstairs. I thought Mom and Dad would be there, but it was quiet. *They were probably being old and went to bed early*, I thought. It was only a little after nine thirty.

I walked over to my car in the driveway, and I thought I saw someone at the corner of my eye, but no one was there when I looked around. I shrugged it off and drove over to the Dumas'. When I got there, I called Ash. She picked up on the second ring.

"Hey girl, how was your Christmas?" she asked in a cheerful voice.

"It was decent. Are you okay?"

"Yeah, I'm fine. I think I might have had a little too much wine, and I'll regret it in the morning, but besides that I'm great." She chuckled. Instead of sounding like cool, calm Ash, she sounded like fiery Ang. Ash wasn't one to drink when upset, but maybe something really bad had happened.

"I'm outside. Can you let me in, or should I call Ang?" I asked.

She was quiet for a few seconds. I started to walk over to the front door from my car.

"I'll be right there," Ash replied.

When I got to the door, she stood in the opening, regarding me curiously. She closed the door behind me, and we both just stared at each other for a moment. Before Ash could say anything, Ang and Mrs. Dumas came from the kitchen. Ang had her hair up in a pretty, messy bun that showed off the sharp edges of her face, which also displayed her shock when she saw me standing in the foyer.

"Hey Rach, you okay?" she asked.

"Oh, Rachel! It's so good to see you! Come, have some dessert," Mrs. Dumas gushed, pulling me into the dining room as Ash and Ang watched me closely.

After dessert, I was quickly escorted upstairs by the twins. When we got to their room, and the door was shut, the interrogation began.

"Okay, so what's going on?" Ang asked.

"That's what I want to know. What's going on Ash?" I asked.

"Me? You came here unannounced. I thought something happened with your parents and Nicole tonight," Ash said.

"Oh yeah, how did that go?" Ang asked.

"It was okay. My Dad still needs some time," I said.

"Okay, so what's wrong? Is this about Kadeem?" Ash asked.

I paused for a moment. I had been doing so well not thinking about that complete shit show for a whole two hours. I exhaled, shaking my head as a response.

"You texted me, Ash," I said, showing her my phone.

"I didn't send that," Ash retorted.

"Well, you *were* drinking," Ang accused.

Ash rolled her eyes at her sister and took a glimpse of her phone. On the screen was a message from her. Her eyebrows furrowed in confusion.

"I guess I did?" she questioned, unsure.

"So everyone is good? Because if that's the case, I'll just go home." I shrugged.

"Rach, it's eleven at night. Crash here and leave in the morning," Ash offered, nudging my knee.

I said, "Okay, sounds good. As long as we don't have to speak about Kadeem tonight."

"We'll just force it out of you in the morning." Ang chuckled, pulling me in for a hug.

Chapter 10

Rachel

I woke up to the sound of sirens blaring in the distance the next morning. Hearing sirens wasn't that strange in a dense area like New York, but usually everyone started to pay attention once the sound didn't fade away. It sounded like the firetrucks kept coming and coming. I finally sat up and rubbed my eyes. I felt Ash shuffling on the other side of the bed too. We both silently made our way over to her window, and that's when I saw it. There was a huge cloud of smoke darkening the already dark, gray sky. It couldn't have been any later than seven in the morning.

"Oh my gosh," Ash gasped.

My brain was still waking up, so I just watched in confusion as I tried to think about why that particular area meant something to me. I had looked at this spot, at this angle, at this distance from Ashlyn's window. Ang burst into our room at that moment, which made Ash and me jump. We both turned to look at her, she had an alarming expression on her face.

"What's wrong? You saw the fire?" Ash asked.

"Rach, I... I just got a call from Alex," Ang faltered.

"Ramos? What did he say?" I asked.

"He said that it's your house... Some explosion or something happened last night–" she began, and I immediately pushed past her.

I threw on my boots and fleece and ran to my car. I sped in the direction of my house, only to be stopped by a police officer when I had gotten closer. I stopped my car in front of the barricade of cop cars and ran over. I patted my pocket for my phone to start calling Mom and Dad. There was no answer. Tears pooled in my eyes when I got close enough to see the damage. The only house that I had known my entire life was a shell of what it used to be. The majority of the rooms, or what used to be rooms were still on fire. I looked at the driveway and saw that both my parents' cars were still there, damaged.

I frantically pushed past the crowd of neighbors and journalists to find them. My chest felt so heavy, my breaths were so labored. Not enough air. I couldn't find them. I started calling and texting them again. All of a sudden, I felt a hand on my shoulder. I jumped. Michelle Solomon stood behind me in a robe and silk pajamas. Her droopy eyes were very concerning, and it made my stomach drop.

"Have you seen my parents? I can't find them," I said, out of breath.

"Um, no, I haven't," she said uneasily.

"Where should I look? Should I see if there's an ambulance or something around here?" I asked.

Michelle skipped a beat before she opened her mouth to answer me, but that's when I saw Ash and Ang running up the block. Ash had tears in her eyes and engulfed me in a hug. I patted her back before turning around to look at Michelle for answers.

"I'm really sorry, Rachel, but I don't think they've found them yet," she said.

Everything froze at that moment. Ang was saying something, but I couldn't hear. The air was extra thick. I could not breathe. I pushed past the girls, storming toward a firefighter who stood closer to the house. I prayed that he would tell me where my parents were.

"Hi, sir, have you seen my parents? They lived in this house," I said, feeling a pang of pain at the word *lived* because there was no way we could live here now.

"Miss, we haven't been able to find anyone yet," he replied.

I saw two firemen run out of the house before an unsettling crunch sounded from the house. The house began to collapse. First, the roof and then the top floor and then our first floor. My home, the memories… just gone. Everyone gasped. Screamed. I felt myself being pulled back toward the street, but all I could do was stare at where my house used to be. *This couldn't be happening. How did this happen?*

Here is what they said happened:

A gas fire was to blame for the destruction of the Smith residence. The fire started in the basement, and even after the fire had spread to the first floor, neighbors did not notice until it was too late, due to the hour it had occurred. There were two casualties as the result of the fire–Jasmine and Malcolm Smith. Their bodies were unable to be recovered.

I finally collected my things from Ash's room and drove to Soteria, where I knew my sister, my only family now, would be. I tried to call her three times during my trip upstate, but it was only ten, and she probably went to bed pretty late because of her drive. Maybe it was best because I probably wouldn't be able to drive once I heard her cry. That would be my undoing. I wiped my eyes as I drove past the mountains, willing myself to take deep breaths and not lose it on the road.

After almost two hours of me using every ounce of my strength to get to the house, I parked my car in the gravel driveway and walked up to the door. I was about to knock when the door opened. Josh opened the door with narrowed eyes and a smirk. I fell into him, and he reached out to catch me. His amused face fell into one of concern as I started to shiver.

"What's wrong, Ray? Talk to me," he said urgently.

"Where's Nicole? I need her," I whispered.

"She's sleeping. She came in after midnight and didn't go to bed until like three. What's going on?" Noah appeared from the kitchen.

"There was a fire. The house is gone," I said, feeling the tears pour from my eyes.

I felt Josh's muscles stiffen. Noah's stoic expression faltered into a look of shock. His eyes moved to the open door behind me and then back at me.

"Where are your parents?" he asked, his voice cautious.

"They're… they didn't make it," I whispered, and it took everything within me to make those words come out.

Noah's eyes closed for a second before he started to take a few steps back. He turned and ran up the stairs.

Eliza came out of the kitchen slowly, and by her expression, I could tell she either heard or came to the right conclusion. She just joined Josh in hugging me.

"I'm so sorry," she soothed, and that made the tears flow more.

They moved me to the couch in the living room. That's when I heard my sister's voice. She spoke harshly, and I could hear her walk down the stairs with heavy steps, which was so abnormal for her. She appeared at the entrance of the room in a tank top and shorts. Her eyes locked with mine in question, as if she needed me to confirm what she'd just heard. I nodded.Her shoulders dropped. Before the rest of her could follow, Noah pulled her over to the other couch, placing her on his lap.

"I'm sorry, Nikki, baby. I'm so, so sorry," he whispered to her softly, but we all could hear.

The next morning, I woke up in a guest room that I didn't have a memory of traveling to. I was still in the clothes I had driven up in. My duffle bag sat on the chair by the window, and there was a faint smell of smoke on my body. That's when the harsh wave of memories from the previous day crashed in.

It felt like there were a dozen bricks being laid on top of my chest, and it was slowly starting to collapse. I took a huge gasp of air, but it didn't help. For a moment, I thought that would be the end of me—just gasping for air, but it soon subsided.

Chapter 11

Rachel

I wasn't sure what day it was when I finally took a shower and walked downstairs to the kitchen. I had a faint memory of someone bringing me water, but that had been about it. I knew I needed food, even if I didn't feel hungry and wanted to keep sleeping. When I slept, I could escape my reality, and at that moment, and *I'm sure you figured this out*, my reality sucked.

"Good morning," Josh's voice pulled me from my thoughts. He was sitting across from Eliza, her eyes sad.

"Well, don't just look at her, feed her," Eliza instructed after a few beats, and I managed a chuckle.

"You don't have to do that. I can make something myself," I softly protested.

"No worries, Ray," Josh said, already turning on the fire on the stove.

I sat next to Eliza at the kitchen island. Her hair was in a messy bun, and I realized it was the first time I saw her where she didn't have the appearance as one would on the cover of *Vogue*. She was still beautiful, of course, but she looked… *normal*.

"Where's Nicole?" I asked.

Josh passed an unreadable look to Eliza before he glanced down to the pan. Eliza stared into her coffee with pursed lips.

"She's out with Noah setting up arrangements with the funeral home," Josh answered.

"Okay, I didn't forget about what happened. What's with the looks?" I asked, glancing between the both of them.

"She hasn't been sleeping much," Eliza confessed after a few beats.

"Well, it's only been a day. Once I start helping her—" I began, but I stopped when Josh turned to me with furrowed eyebrows.

"It's been three," he said.

I immediately reached for his phone and realized that it was the twenty-ninth. A feeling of disorientation started to creep up on me. I was about to ask them why I hadn't been woken up, but then we heard the front door open. Nicole walked through with a coffee cup in her hand and her phone in the other. On the surface, she only looked a little worn out, but I knew my sister, and she wasn't okay.

"Hey," I said, hopping off my stool and taking a few steps toward her.

"Morning," Nicole answered coldly, continuing to tap on her screen with great speed.

I slowly turned to Noah leaning against the closed front door. He pursed his lips into a frown, his eyes securely on my sister. Something was wrong. I raised an eyebrow at him, but he just kept his head down as he walked into the kitchen.

"How are you?" I asked.

Nicole gave me a blank stare for a few seconds before turning her attention back to her phone. I didn't know what to think of that and settled into silence for a second. *Did something else happen? Something no one wants to address?*

"Do you want some breakfast now?" Josh asked.

"No, I have my coffee," Nicole answered shakily before putting her phone to her ear and walking into the office room.

My sister *never* drank coffee. She also was not the biggest fan of breakfast, but her drinking coffee instead of tea confirmed that something was very wrong. Josh called my name, holding my plate in the air..

"Eat, please," he mouthed.

After breakfast, I asked Nicole what I could help with. She shrugged and told me everything was almost done, but I could take a look at the slideshow to see if I wanted to add any more pictures.

"Did you do this all yourself?" I asked.

"Most of it, yes," she said.

"Have you slept?"

"Why are you asking so many questions?"

"Because you have to be tired," I said.

"I'm fine," she waved me off.

"When was the last time you slept?" I asked after a few beats.

"Why?" She glanced up from her phone this time.

Whenever Nicole answered my questions with questions, it was never good. I sighed inwardly at the thought of her not having slept for the past few days and me not even being checked in enough to be there for her.

"You're making all these calls and doing stuff. I want to make sure you're taking care of yourself too," I said.

"I'm planning their funeral because who else is going to do it?" Nicole asked firmly.

Her eyes could've cut glass. *Was her anger pointed towards me?* My stomach turned, and my pulse intensified.

"Nicole, something is wrong with you," I choked out.

"I told you—"

"Seriously, what's wrong? You seem off."

She threw her cell phone down on the table and rubbed her temples. It was the most animated thing I'd seen her do the whole morning.

"Rachel, please leave me alone," she said.

"But I just want you to talk to me!" I screamed.

"And what the fuck do you want me to say? *That I'm sad?* That I didn't get to spend time with them before they died? That that's your fault? That I have a lot of shit to do all the time, and I can't even deal with my own emotions? That my life isn't my own? That I chose for it to be this way and now there's no way out? That my youth is literally fleeting, and I'll never get to actually enjoy it? That nothing has been able to make me happy lately? Is that what you want me to say? Because now I did, and look at you, you can't even handle it!" She sobbed.

I tried to hug her, but she put out her arm to stop me. Then she looked up with tears flooding her eyes. She wasn't looking at me, but behind me. Noah stood in the doorway. His expression, devastated.

"Noah, I didn't–" she began.

"Greg said he was able to figure out the florist situation," Noah said coldly, walking away.

"Noah, wait, please," Nicole called, standing from her seat.

He shook his head and held his hand out. "I'm going for a walk."

Nicole didn't follow him, but instead, walked past me and upstairs.

I woke up to noise in the kitchen. I had fallen asleep on the couch. Sitting up, I saw Noah eating mac and cheese from one of those microwavable cups. He stared straight at the fridge in silence. I didn't think he noticed me until he began to speak.

"Sorry if I woke you," he apologized in a low voice, not even glancing my way.

"It's okay. What time is it anyway?" I asked.

"Like two in the morning," he surmised.

"Why are you up?"

"Because," he replied, which wasn't really an answer, but for some reason it made perfect sense.

"I'm sorry about earlier with Nicole," I finally said.

He grunted in response and blinked really slowly.

"Do you hate me too?" I asked, which finally broke his trance and made him face me.

"Never," he said softly, his facial expression telling he thought the idea was ridiculous.

"I'm sure you hate me sometimes. Even my own sister hates me sometimes," I said.

"No, I hate my mom. I hate my uncle. I hate the assholes at The Table, but I don't hate you. Not you, Rachel," he said.

"Please don't break up with my sister." At that moment, I felt vulnerable enough to start blurting out things that were worrying me.

"*Oh, don't worry I won't,*" he said, chuckling. "The only way out of this is one of us dying. I love Nicole, and I'll just have to figure out a way to make her happy."

"But what she said earlier about not being happy, and you hearing it…" I trailed off.

"Yeah, I know. I'd like to say being married means that shit like that doesn't happen, but it does. We still love each other, despite things being hard right now."

I noticed his sad smile, tired eyes, and shadow of a beard. I wanted to hug him. Instead, tears started to fall from my eyes. Noah walked over and pulled me in for a hug.

"Rachel, just give it time. It'll be okay," he said.

"I'm a bad sister," I choked.

"No you're not."

"I am. I stayed in bed for like three days and left her to do this on her own. Plus, she feels like she didn't get to spend time with them recently because of me," I said, surprised I was still holding onto him, but nothing made sense these days anyway.

"Rachel, you don't grieve in a way that's convenient for everyone else. You gotta do what you gotta do. Nicole just needs some time," he comforted.

"I'm glad Nicole has you," I said into his chest after a moment.

"Thanks for always being my family," he whispered.

"Since when did you become a softy?" I chuckled.

"Your sister melted my ice a little. Only a little, though," he said, and I could imagine the rare smile on his face.

The next morning, I woke to a knock on my door. I grumbled in response, but the knocking persisted. Finally, I yelled for the person to come in. Josh walked in dressed in pajama pants and a t-shirt. His expression looked very unsure as if he wasn't sure he would just see me peeking out from under my covers.

"Morning," he said.

"Hey, what's up?" I asked in the whisper my throat would only allow.

"I wanted to see how you were. I know today is the day," he said.

I pushed myself upward to lean on the plush headboard. It was clearly not a sunny day out, but there was enough light coming through the windows to let me know it was well into the morning. It wouldn't be long until the thing that I had been dreading would happen. I took a deep breath and let it out slowly.

"I don't know. I just want to skip today,"

"I understand," he said.

"No, you don't," I sighed, getting upset.

Josh stared for a moment before he walked over and sat on the foot of my bed. His glasses were off, and the light of the sunrise danced with the variants of color in his eyes. His jaw worked as he played with a thread on the comforter.

"For years, I had to try to process the fact that my parents were gone. Initially, I didn't even know what death meant. I just knew I hadn't seen them in a while, and then, as time went on, I realized it was more permanent. It may not have been true, but it was reality for the time being," he said.

"I'm sorry," I said.

"Don't be. You didn't mean any harm." He shrugged.

"I should just shut up sometimes." I slipped out of the covers and walked over to the bathroom.

"Ray, it's really fine. You're hurting right now," he called loud enough for me to hear behind the mostly closed door.

"I guess that's what I'm feeling. I just want to not feel this way," I admitted after a couple minutes.

"Well, today will be hard, but you know what the good thing about after that is?" He purposely averted his eyes to the ceiling when he realized I was pulling my shirt down to cover the fact that I didn't have pants on. His eyes found me again when I was under the fluffy, white comforter. He laid across the bottom of the bed and turned to look at me.

"I won't have to sit here waiting for the funeral to be over?" I took a guess.

"That and after today, you can focus on working through the pain instead of everything else."

I couldn't tell you what happened during the funeral service. It was almost as if I was elsewhere, floating above my body. I know I was there, I remember that. I know that I somehow ended up at the cemetery. For probably many reasons, I couldn't remember the ride there. The haze didn't start to dissipate until we were all standing around the two caskets that were being suspended over two plots. Some of our family members said some words similar to those they probably said at the funeral.

Nicole stood to the left of me, and to her left, Noah. Josh had been by my side since the beginning of the service. I did remember that part. He was there to help me walk in my heels and was there to hold my hand when I needed it. Joshua Crawford was a good friend, and I didn't have the words to say it, but I really appreciated him.

"I'll be right back. There's a few old ladies who need help with walking on the grass," he whispered, patting my shoulder.

"Okay," I nodded.

He gave me a small smile before he turned and walked across the grass in his long black coat and suit. I looked over to Nicole, but she was whispering to Noah who wrapped his arms around her. I felt someone standing next to me again, and I thought it was Josh, but it was a white woman with a long sleek black braid. She wore a very wide brimmed hat and large sunglasses. She appeared equally as ominous as she did glamorous. She turned toward me when she saw me looking at her.

"I'm sorry, do I know you?" I asked softly.

"Maybe not, but I certainly know who you are," she said, taking a step toward me in her long black coat.

"Who are you?" I asked after a moment, assuming she was a neighbor or something.

"I just wanted to share my deepest condolences to you and your family," she said.

"Thank you."

"I can't believe it happened this way. I mean, you could have easily been caught in that fire too. You left just in time, actually," she said.

"I… suppose," I stammered, a little put off by the statement.

"It's a shame that you couldn't bring them with you. You must think about that all the time," she continued.

"Excuse me, who are you, again?" I asked, no longer wanting to hear any of this. Some people really didn't know what to say to those who were grieving.

The woman slid down her glasses for a moment, and when I saw her face, I immediately knew who she was. Tracey Crawford.

"Oh Rachel, you escaped me twice with your car and your house, but this is only the beginning," the woman uttered smugly.

"What are you talking about? Di– Did you have something to do with the fire?" I asked louder than I intended.

"She's smart, just like her sister," Tracey sighed.

"Rachel, what's wrong? Why do you look like that?" Josh asked, walking back to me. He curiously eyed the back of Tracy's head.

"Oh no, Rachel, you don't look so good. If it makes you feel any better, it was supposed to be you, not them. Consider yourself lucky, for now," Tracey said.

"Mother, why are you here?" I heard Noah's voice ask behind me before he and Nicole appeared in my field of vision. His eyebrows were furrowed intensely like he already knew.

"Look who it is, it's my son and his concubine," Tracey announced, much louder than a whisper.

"Alright, it's time for you to leave," Josh advised, his voice stern, so unlike his usual tone.

Tracey's eyebrows raised beyond the mask of her sunglasses, and she crossed her arms with a smirk. It was then I noticed two men who were the size of tanks standing nearby with their hands on something underneath their suit jackets.

"He speaks," she said. "You know, I know all about you Joshua Westbrook, or should I say *Crawford*. I'd be very careful. Your tone is inappropriate."

"Security! Please escort Ms. Tracey Crawford out and off the premises," I heard Greg say into his phone as he walked up to the crowd that was forming, Eliza behind him.

"I'm leaving, anyway. I'm just here to remind you that your era of peace is over, like I told you before," she said, putting on her lace black gloves.

She walked away, disappearing into the low fog that blanketed the cemetery. I started to shiver and couldn't stop. Josh hugged me, encouraging tears to stream out of me as I buried my face in his chest. I felt someone's hand rub my back and was unsure of who it was until I heard Eliza's voice. She said something, but I couldn't get myself to ask her to repeat herself. All I could do was cry.

Chapter 12

Josh

I had never been to a funeral before. I'd seen them take place countless times on TV, but those had nothing on the funeral that was held for the Smiths. I felt so many emotions over the course of the day, and while I had only known Jasmine and Malcolm Smith for a short time, I knew I would miss them. I knew that the pain their daughters felt was immeasurable and surpassed what I felt in every way. They both had held their composure until the caskets started to lower into the ground.

Nicole was the first one to break. Her scream was guttural when they first started to descend. Noah had put back on his sunglasses, but I could see his tears running past the lens as he held her up. Rachel started to shake intensely, but we both held onto each other. I felt tears pooling in my eyes, so I exhaled, trying to hold it back. I felt someone's hand on my back, and it was Jason behind me. His eyes were red, and Eliza stood next to him with a hand on his arm. Even though it was under the most undesirable circumstances, I will never forget how connected we were with each other that day.

We all went to Noah's Queens apartment that evening after the events of the very long, unfortunate day. Nicole and Noah went out onto the balcony to speak privately with skyscrapers as their backdrop. Jason sat at the kitchen, glued to his phone, bags forming beneath his eyes. Eliza rested her eyes, lounging on a chair. Rachel also napped, but instead of a chair like Eliza, she napped with her head resting on my lap. I had covered her with my suit jacket, and for the first time all day, she looked at peace. That was worth having to stay still.

Noah walked back inside, leaving Nicole on the balcony with his jacket over her shoulders. He stopped when he saw Rachel sleeping, the expression on his face held a conglomerate of emotions. His eyes lingered on us for a long moment before he walked into the kitchen. He patted Jason on the shoulder on his way to look inside his refrigerator. I knew what the look was for, and I was brought back to reality as I looked down at Rachel still peacefully sleeping.

***

It was Rachel's birthday. I was surprised she invited me to hang out with her friends, but of course, I was happy to go. Unsure of what to get her, I finally settled on something I thought she would enjoy.

"Must I open all my gifts in front of everyone?" Rachel rolled her eyes.

"Yes! Now open mine," Angelica, Rachel's friend, exclaimed before handing her a gift bag.

"Fine!" Rachel laughed.

She excitedly opened the gift to reveal a custom-made jacket that featured their college's logo. She put it on, and it fit her perfectly. Rachel squealed with excitement and hugged Angelica. Next, she opened Ashlyn's gift. She had gotten her a handbag that Rachel modeled around for a moment. Nicole got Rachel a necklace with two dancing shoes in the pendant. Rachel hugged her lovingly, and I watched everyone light up at the sight.

Soon, it was my turn to give her my gift. I handed her the gift bag. When she pulled the frame out, her face beamed with an amused smile. She turned the frame around, and it was a sketch of a map of New York City with a zig-zag trail.

"It's a map of when you showed me around New York City for the first time," I said.

"I know! You clowned me about how insane the day was for weeks. I didn't know you kept the trail our phone mapped out." Rachel laughed.

"Of course, but I still had the best time. This is just so you have documentation of your work." I chuckled.

She hopped off her seat and jumped on me to wrap her arms around my neck. I looked down to see her feet dangling and hugged her back.

"Thank you, Joshy," Rachel said.

"That's so sweet. I love that," Ashlyn added.

I noticed everyone agreeing besides Noah, who was leaning against the back wall staring at me. Giving him a questioning raise of a brow, he gestured for me to follow him. When we made it into another room, he closed the door.

"You okay, man?" I asked.

"You're insane," he accused.

"Excuse me?"

"Just know that if you cross that line, I will have to kick your ass if you hurt her," he said.

"What? What are you talking about? Who?"

"You're in love with Rachel. Nicole will probably slaughter you before I even have a chance."

My jaw dropped, and I started to laugh. I was *not* in love with Rachel. There wasn't a reason. I mean, yes, she was gorgeous, intelligent, and the funniest person I knew, but that did not mean I was in love with her.

"No, I'm not," I retorted.

"Josh, I have eyes."

"What? What are you seeing besides two people being friends?"

"Right..."

"I'm so confused," I breathed.

"Damn, you don't even realize it yet. Just remember what I said–that's Nicole's sister. I don't want to kick your ass." Noah scowled.

"Um, okay," I said before he left the room.

***

I thought about setting her on the couch because of his words, but at the same time, I didn't want to. Even with the so-called-warning Noah gave me, I just didn't want to push her away. And so, I didn't. I pulled my jacket over her shoulder and rested content, knowing that at least she could escape the reality of what was going on.

Rachel and Nicole had decided to stay in New York, even though several family members offered to have them move in with them. Boston, Seattle, and Los Angeles were just some of the cities they had the option to live in, but they decided to stay here. I selfishly felt at ease knowing that they had decided to stay right before the funeral. In the days following the funeral, Nicole and Noah bought a bigger apartment in the building that they'd rented an apartment in for school. Rachel was off from school for the next few weeks and silently decided to come upstate to get some space and quiet. Soteria was huge, and she could get virtually everything she needed up there.

It was so strange not hearing her make any sassy remarks or hear her laugh. On our car ride up there, we sat next to each other in silence. The only speaking I did was when Greg asked a question from the front seat. He wanted to drive us up this time. I noticed his eyes glancing over at her from time to time, and it was obvious that even he missed hearing Rachel's voice. Still, I was happy to be there for her.

When we got to the house, Caesar greeted us and told Rachel that he had someone buy her some new clothes because he knew she would need some. She gave him a thankful nod and started to head upstairs.

"We left the receipts just in case you would like to exchange them, Ms. Rachel. Mr. Noah said that you can get whatever you want," he called after her.

When she had disappeared from sight, he slowly turned back to me with a worried frown.

"Has she spoken since the funeral?" he asked quietly so only I could hear.

"No," I replied in equal volume.

"When our brother died, my sister didn't speak for two months," he said, and I could see the pain in his eyes.

"That's a long time. What made her speak again?"

"Nothing in particular, I think. She just needed time. Rachel needs time too," he said.

"I just feel bad. I don't know how to help her."

"I think you should just keep doing what you're doing," he said, patting my shoulder.

"But I haven't done anything."

"You have, trust me, Joshua," he said with a smile.

For the next couple weeks, I barely saw Rachel. I would check up on her twice a day, but I knew that she wanted to be alone. In the late mornings, I would check to see if she ate anything. Most of the time, she would nod and point to a smoothie or a small plate of something. Other times, she would shake her head no and sink back under the covers. For those mornings, I would leave a snack and a bottle of water on her nightstand for when she was ready. Right before bed, I would check to see what she was doing and see if she needed anything. Sometimes she would be sleeping and other times she was swiping on her phone. I always asked if she needed anything, but she always shook her head no.

After the two week mark, I got tired of working out extra to waste time or even playing video games. How ironic was it that I wanted to do something else different than what I normally did just because she was in the house? I walked over to her bedroom, knocked twice before opening the door, but when I opened it, she wasn't in there.

"Rachel?" I called down the hallway, but I knew she wasn't going to answer.

"She's down here," another familiar female voice called.

I walked downstairs to see Eliza and Rachel sitting across from each other on the kitchen island with a small dry-erase board in between them. They were both dressed in heavy sweaters and boots like they had recently come in from outside.

"Morning, pretty boy. How's it going?" Eliza asked.

"Good, you know, taking it one day at a time. How are you? Everything *Gucci*?" I asked, letting my attention bounce between the two of them.

"Ha, Gucci. It's American Eagle at best, maybe even Walmart, but we're pushing through," she exhaled deeply.

"Why?" I asked.

"Because school is coming up, and that means the spring semester of my junior year begins, which means I have to start planning my senior project, and I don't have any idea on what I would like to do," she said.

"You're an English major, right?" I asked.

"Yup," she responded.

"Maybe a paper or a website about something you like?" I suggested.

"I can pretty much do anything, but I want it to be exciting. Anyway, this is totally a me problem. I'll figure it out over the next few months. I just came up here to get some inspiration and check up on everyone," she said, looking at Rachel.

Rachel gave her a small smile and wrote "thank you" on the board. Eliza smiled back at her. Eliza's narrowed eyes examined me curiously before she announced that they would be taking a walk. I was happy that Rachel would have someone else to talk to. I excused myself when my phone began to ring. It was Mom.

"Hey," I answered, walking into the living room.

"Good morning, Joshua. How are you? How are the girls?" she asked softly.

"I'm alright. Rachel and Nicole are getting through it. One step at a time, right?" I said.

"Jason told me that you were taking care of Rachel. She hasn't been speaking," she continued.

"Yeah, it's been hard for her," I said, unsure if I should delve into what happened before she stopped speaking.

"I hope she finds comfort in the thought that they're safe now," she replied, which made me pause.

"Safe? They're dead," I reminded her.

"Uh, well, yeah… Okay, so I shouldn't use the word *safe*. They are now at peace. They are no longer feeling pain. I hope that brings her comfort. That is what I meant."

Chapter 13

Rachel

It was as if something in me broke when they lowered the caskets in the ground. I almost passed out, but Josh held me upright. I couldn't tell you any details about the day beyond that. I think my brain blocked all of them out to protect me. Some days I wish I could remember more, and other days… Well, I'm grateful that I couldn't relive the day even if I tried. Some days shouldn't be lived once, let alone twice.

What I do remember is that I stopped speaking. I guess it was from the shock of it all. I didn't completely realize until a couple weeks into my stay at Soteria. Eliza walked into my room and sat on the foot of my bed with a marker and a little dry erase board. She handed the two items to me with a hopeful gleam in her eyes.

"I think we all miss hearing your voice, but until you are ready, we can use this," she said.

I nodded slowly in response, grateful that she was there.

"What would you like for lunch? Caesar said he can get the cook to make whatever you want. When I texted

Josh, he said you didn't eat much yesterday, and you really should," she suggested kindly. It was almost foreign coming from her.

I exhaled sharply. I didn't want to eat, but I knew she was right. I wrote down a simple chicken sandwich to appease everyone. She nodded at the board and gave me a small smile, pleased.

"It's a little warmer today. Would you like to go out and do something?" she asked.

I didn't need to write down anything for that one. I shook my head to say no. Eliza frowned before stretching out on the foot of my bed. She was so tall and limby, like a model. I wondered if that's what helped give her an intimidating aura. Maybe that and the condescending scowl she gave time-to-time. She didn't have that look this time, though. She seemed genuinely concerned.

"Come on, it'll be good for you. I won't make you talk. I hate the quiet, but I guess I can endure it for a little bit," she said with a wink.

I found myself scribbling a question on the board. "Why do you hate the quiet?"

She bit her lip as she paused. "When things are quiet, I have to finally face the things that I try to avoid, you know? Anyway, that got a little dark, and now you owe me a walk. Get dressed, Little Smith. I'll be ready in twenty minutes."

Eliza and I walked in silence for some time. I kind of just wandered, losing track of time. Surprisingly, I liked it that way. We got to a spot where we could get a good view of the river. We both just stared at it for a while.

"How's Kadeem?" Eliza asked, breaking the silence.

I shrugged in response. I really didn't know, and I really did not care.

"Should I kick his ass?" she asked.

I nodded with a small smile, and she chuckled. I put my middle fingers up toward the river. Eliza smirked and nodded in approval. At that moment, I thought to myself about how we probably could have been friends if she wasn't mean to Nicole sometimes. Nicole and I had spoken about it several times. My pacifist sister told me that Eliza had been through a lot of pain, and the least she could do was be understanding of that. I hadn't come to that conclusion yet, but right then, I was happy that she was there.

"You know, Little Smith, you and your sister are some of the most beautiful women I know. I mean it. If that asshole doesn't realize how lucky he is to be wanted by you, then you dodged the bullet of dating an idiot," she said frankly.

I wanted to thank her and say so much in response, but instead, I nodded. A cold wind blew, and her auburn hair whirled around her. She slid her hands into her coat pockets, closing her eyes for a moment like she was processing something, trying to feel something. With her eyes shut, it gave me the opportunity to just stare at her, and I realized that Elizabeth Craig *was* a woman who carried a lot of pain. I knew right then that I would try my best not to be yet another source of it. Nicole would be proud.

"Why aren't you talking to anyone?" Eliza finally asked after a while.

I just looked at her. I'm not sure what my face expressed, but it seemed to answer something for her because her next question caught me off guard.

"What did Tracey say to you? Did she do something?"

Exhaling deeply, I looked down at my boots, sliding my hands in my pockets. All of a sudden, it felt really cold. My body started shivering like it did at the funeral. Eliza turned to me, placing her hands on my shoulders.

"Okay, look at me," she demanded, her voice firm.

I lifted my chin. Stared at her as I tried to focus on not trembling.

"Nod or shake your head to my questions. Did Tracey have something to do with the fire?" Eliza asked, but it sounded like she already knew the answer.

I nodded. Tears burned behind my eyes..

"Did she say something else?"

I nodded again.

"Hmm, did she say why she did it?"

Nod.

"Did… she want to kill you or your parents?"

I let out a wail. My finger pressed against my chest. Eliza's eyes widened, and she pulled me in for a hug. My face hidden by her coat, she rubbed my back until I was able to find air again.

I found Josh reading a book by a window seat in the house one early morning a few days later. It was in the attic, and I had only found it after exploring one late afternoon when it seemed like everyone either decided to take a nap or be by themselves. I wasn't sure why, but I stood there for a while, observing him. The sun was rising, and its light formed a halo behind him. His hair had started to grow back in again, and I couldn't decide which look I liked on him more. After a few moments, I decided he was one of those guys who looked equally as fine with both.

"Hi," he said, and I realized he was gazing right at me.

I jumped a little, causing him to smile. He shifted to the side and patted the space next to him. I crossed the room and sat next to him.

"How are you?" he asked.

I tilted my head from side to side as I observed the room. Lines of books decorated shelves, along with the old toys and a computer that was stored in the room.

Josh's gaze followed mine. "Yeah, I keep some of my old stuff in here. Sometimes I escape here to read and just be alone. I thought after all these years of being alone I would never miss it, but I do. While some find discomfort in the silence, I see it as a luxury that should not go overlooked. Seems like the secret's out though," he teased with a chuckle.

I turned, frowning at him apologetically, standing up to leave. He reached out and gently grabbed onto my arm.

"I didn't say I didn't like that you found it too," he said, and I sat down again.

He stared at me for a second, and I stared back like there was some mutual understanding. I had no idea what it was, but I would figure it out eventually. His hazel eyes were alive in the light. Josh was an attractive guy, even though he annoyed me sometimes. Over anything though, he was a good person, and I smiled at the thought. I didn't often think about the little things with people, but after some of the big things were gone, I found myself appreciating them more.

"What?" he asked.

I shook my head.

"You know, I never thought I would say this, but I can't wait until you're ready to speak again. As much as you like to get on my nerves, I miss it." He chuckled as he closed his book and placed the bookmark back in the pages carefully.

I smiled with my teeth that time. It was the first time I had done that in what seemed like weeks. Josh laughed quietly, lifting a hand. For a moment, it looked as if he was going to reach for my face, but I brushed away the thought, realizing I must've misread the way his hands moved.

"Let's keep this place our secret, okay? I don't want the others to infiltrate. It will never be peaceful again," he said.

I gave him my pinkie, and he slowly wrapped his around mine.

Chapter 14

Josh

My phone started to ring with Noah's name across the top of the screen. I told Nina that I was taking a ten minute break before our next round, and she agreed with a nod on my screen. I muted my mic before tapping on my phone.

"Hey brother," I answered.

"Hey, how's Rachel?" Noah asked.

"She's okay. Not really saying much, but she's okay."

"Nicole's not happy that she decided to take the semester online."

"Well, it makes sense if she's not going to participate in class," I pointed out.

"Yeah, I know. I think she's just worried about her."

"How is Nicole anyway?"

"She's staying busy. Much better than a few weeks ago, but I don't think she wants to talk about it yet," Noah said.

"I see." I couldn't blame her—I probably wouldn't want to either, if I was in her position.

"I've also spoken with Eliza. She found out that Tracey caused the fire. Her target was Rachel, not the Smiths. So, please keep an eye out. I'm sending Greg to take a look at the security systems and make sure everything looks okay," Noah said.

"Great, another thing to worry about," I sighed.

"Also," Noah continued.

"Also?" I groaned, rubbing my forehead.

"You are legally required to attend a meeting with The Table in the next couple months. I don't have a date yet. There's some legal kinks, but yeah, that's a thing too."

"And I thought this was a friendly wellness check," I curtly replied.

"Hey, listen, this is not me. I believe my mother has something to do with this shit," he said.

"Okay, well, I'm going to get off the phone before you throw anything else at me," I snorted.

"Josh," he said sternly.

"Yeah?"

"Take care of her."

That afternoon, I found Rachel typing on her laptop in the living room. She had earbuds in and didn't notice me standing there. I waved my arm in an exaggerated way like people do in a crowd on TV, and she slowly looked up.

"Hey, just letting you know Caesar said he's going to make steak. I figured that was fine, right?" I asked.

She nodded with a small smile. I smiled back and left her alone.

After dinner, I sat in the living room and watched the flames in the fireplace flicker and spark. I heard the front door open and close quietly. I didn't turn around. I assumed that I knew who it was.

"Hey Greg," I called.

There was no answer. I turned around. No one was there. *That was strange*, I thought. I stood up, expecting to see Caesar putting something in the trash or a maid leaving late for the day, but there was no one. I walked past the office when I saw someone standing there in the dark. I turned on the light. A man stood dressed in black with a gun pointed in my direction. I froze. Shit.

I put my hands up. I started to think of so many things at once. The main two were how would Rachel and I get out of this alive, and how anyone made it in with the security system being on.

"What do you want?" I asked carefully.

"Listen, kid, it's not personal. Let's not make this any harder than it needs to be," the man replied.

"Josh behind you!" I heard Rachel's voice scream, and I turned around to see someone with a bat just about to swing, but I moved just in time.

The gun went off, but I didn't feel anything. Instead, the man with a bat hollered in pain. I ran down the hallway where Rachel stood, her eyes fearful.

"We have to get out of here," I said.

She dragged me to the kitchen and grabbed the biggest knife there. She held her phone on an angle at the edge of the kitchen. I grabbed a knife too and peered out of the kitchen from where I was standing. Then I heard footsteps. Rachel crouched down and swung her arm out. The sound that followed as a loud scream. The gun slid across the floor. I grabbed it. I looked where the man now laid, he crouched with his arm around his stomach.

"Are you okay?" I asked Rachel.

"No, but alive," she said.

"Bravo, Rachel Smith," a familiar voice sounded.

Rachel's expression immediately shifted. As the footsteps descended down the stairs, Tracey Crawford appeared from the shadows.

"What?" The word dropped from my mouth like a bomb.

"Well, well, well… Look who's still alive," Tracey said.

"What do you want?" Rachel asked, and it was still so strange to hear her voice after so many weeks.

"I already told you," Tracey replied coldly.

"Get out of my house," I barked.

Tracey merely glanced at me and laughed. She walked up to me until she was only inches away. Her skin was pale, and she had raven black hair that made her features look hollow.

"Sounds like you're arrogant just like your father," she accused, assessing me with piercing eyes.

"Leave him alone," Rachel warned.

"It's so good you're using your voice again. Josh really missed it," Tracey crooned. Suddenly, I felt my muscles clench. An unrecognizable sound left my mouth, then I was on the ground.

"NO!" Rachel screamed, the word bouncing against the walls.

"Relax. He's only been tased, Rachel. He'll live, for now. But now, I see there's more at stake here…This is very interesting. I'll tell you what," Tracey said before Rachel made a gagging noise and ended up on the ground too.

"Ray," I groaned, trying to reach for her, but I had a hard time moving.

Tracey put her boot on my forearm, and I stopped trying. It didn't necessarily hurt yet, but I knew it could get much worse.

"Why?" I asked breathlessly, looking up at Tracey.

"Now that we're all listening," Tracey smirked, "I want to make this a little more fun."

"How?" Rachel strained.

"I'm going to let you decide who dies," Tracey said cheerfully. It was the most sadistic thing most people would ever imagine hearing.

"What? Why? What's the point?" Rachel urged.

"Well, it would serve the purpose of what I need here. See, Rachel, I almost broke you, but if I killed your little friend here, I know that would be it for you. I can settle for that. Josh, your father refused to kill you on multiple occasions, and you're one of the reasons why he is dead now," she said conversationally.

"What are you talking about?" I pushed myself off the ground until I was able to sit upright.

"I gave him an out before we killed him. I told him we could figure something out if we get rid of one of the major holders in the CCT Network. He refused to tell me where you were. I knew you would finally turn up somewhere. I mean, if you think about it, all of this has happened because of *you*. So you see, both of you just can't seem to die and let things go my way."

"You're fucking sick," Rachel spat.

"Oh, your first words and they're so dirty? I'm going to give you a month to decide who should go. If you don't decide, maybe both of you will have to," Tracey declared.

"You're not going to get away with this, you know," I warned.

"We'll see. Have fun deliberating, you two. I'll be watching," she said before three men appeared from corners of the house and grabbed the two men who had been hurt.

Even after Rachel and I were alone, we sat on the floor for hours in silence.

Chapter 15

Rachel

Josh and I barely spoke to each other, even though we both were too spooked to leave each other's side that night. Any peace that could've been found in the silence was replaced with fear of the unknown. After I showered, I found my way into his room, and we both just stared at the ceiling as we laid back in his bed. My head was on the pillows, his at the foot of the bed.

I wasn't sure if I had fallen asleep or watched the sun rise, but morning came soon enough. Light filtered into the room through the curtains, and we both sat up at the same time. When I looked down at Josh, his drowsy eyes blinked slowly, and he only had on pajama pants. He ran a hand over his face and got up to grab his glasses on the computer desk.

"Good morning," he finally said in a groggy voice.

"Morning," I answered.

"How'd you sleep?" he asked.

"I'm not really sure," I said.

"That's better than not at all, I guess," he said, pulling a shirt over his head.

He sat down at his desk and started tapping on his phone. I scanned the room for mine and saw it on the nightstand on the other side of the bed. There were two missed calls from Nicole. I tapped on her name and waited for her to pick up. It was early, but she probably was awake.

"Where have you been? I tried to call you last night," Nicole answered sternly after the second ring.

"I never heard it. Sorry, uh… Tracey was here last night," I said.

"Shit. She must have access to some signal blocking device. Are you okay? Where's Josh? Where's Greg? We can't reach him," Nicole asked all in one breath, and her high alert energy was pulling me out of the sleepy fog I was in.

"I'm okay, I guess. Josh is here. He's doing decent too. Greg isn't here," I replied.

Suddenly, Josh stood up and cursed under his breath, bringing his phone to his ear. I raised an eyebrow at him as he paced back and forth in the open space in his room.

"What?" I asked him.

"Greg was supposed to be here last night. He never showed up," he breathed.

"Oh no. I wonder if Tracey found him first," I speculated, a million possibilities forming in my mind.

"We're like twenty minutes away," Nicole said through the phone.

"What? Who's us? How did you know to come up here?"

"Because no one answered last night, and Greg's phone is going to voicemail. Noah, Eliza, Jason, and I all tried calling the three of you and couldn't reach you," she said.

"You don't think something bad happened do you?" I asked.

"We don't know," Nicole said.

Just then, the doorbell rang, and Josh and I exchanged a confused glance.

"They're here already?" Josh asked.

Nicole must've heard him through the phone and replied, "No, we're driving. Who is it?"

"I don't know. Hold on," I said.

Josh started making his way downstairs first, and I followed. He looked through the peephole and then quickly opened a door to a really beaten up version of Greg standing at the door. He limped his way in before Josh closed the door and helped him to the couch. His clothes looked damp, and his face was bruised.

"It's Greg. He's pretty bruised up, but he's here," I told Nicole.

"Okay. At least he's alive," Nicole sighed in relief.

"What happened?" Josh asked, kneeling beside him.

"Tracey's crew found me. Knocked me out. My car went out of control and over a cliff. I was able to knock a window out and swim out… Walked about fifteen miles here," he responded, his voice strained and tired.

"Fuck," Josh breathed, and it was so rare to hear him curse out loud, I would have made a point of it if it weren't such a bad time.

"Noah, baby, you have to slow down. You're going to kill us," I heard Nicole say.

"You guys get here safe. Let us know when you're here," I ordered.

"Okay," Nicole said reluctantly before hanging up.

We made Greg a warm cup of coffee and grabbed him some dry clothes to step into by time everyone else made it to the house. Noah was the first one who ran in. His eyes were dark and his eyebrows were tightly drawn as he stormed toward a tired Greg. His anger vibrated the room. Nicole walked in right behind him with Jason, whose face was riddled with concern. The first thing he did was go to hug Josh. Nicole slowly pulled me in for one too. It had been so long since we hugged or really spoke to each other, but it was welcomed.

"I'm sorry," she whispered.

"For what?" I asked.

"For not understanding that you needed to grieve the way you needed to. I love you." She squeezed me, and I rubbed her back in response

Our moment didn't last long. Everyone gathered in the living room.

"So, guys, what the hell happened last night?" Eliza asked.

"Yeah, how did you make it out unmarked?" Greg asked.

"Not unmarked," Josh said, pulling his pajama pants up to show a large bruise on his leg.

Nicole gasped, and Eliza squatted by his leg to get a better look.

"Tased," Eliza confirmed.

"Were you tased too?" Nicole asked, looking at me.

"Yeah, on the back of my thigh," I said, locking eyes with Josh.

"Apparently we have to choose who dies. That's Tracey's deal," Josh explained with a sigh.

"Excuse fucking me?" Eliza exclaimed.

"Yeah, some bullshit about how Carter is dead because he wouldn't kill Josh and how she wants to hurt Nicole so she wants me to die," I said.

"We have to do something. This has gone too far, Noah," Eliza asserted, standing up.

"I don't want anyone getting hurt. I think we should all lay low," Noah said.

"If we lay low, they will die, Noah," Eliza challenged loudly.

"If we go and attack them, we will all die too. Give me some time to figure this out," Noah said.

"But–" Eliza started.

"Eliza, let me do *my* job," Noah growled.

Eliza huffed and stomped out of the room.

"I'm not one to jump on the Eliza train, as she would rather me dead, *but* she has a point, dude," Jason said.

Noah gave Jason an exasperated look, and Jason put his hands up in surrender. Noah walked out the room too. Josh and I looked at each other for a moment. I wanted to cry, but I didn't. Nicole rubbed my arm before she went after Noah. I prayed she would talk some sense into him. Laying low probably wouldn't work this time. Tracey didn't care if we didn't go after her. She was angry about what had already happened.

"Are you guys really okay?" Jason asked after a long pause.

"Okay as we can be," I said.

"Listen, Ray, just so we're clear, if we can't figure this out, I'll go," Josh announced, and I immediately felt as if I were shot.

"No, I won't let you do that. I'll go," I said, taking a step toward him.

"Rachel, you got to let me give you this solid. I won't let them hurt you," he insisted.

"Woah… Okay, I'm going to go and see if anything has been figured out. No one is going to sign off their lives for anyone else, yet," Jason hesitated, slowly backing out of the room.

"It makes more sense if it's me," Josh breathed, very matter-of-fact like he had already accepted his fate. It made my insides hurt again, just like they did months ago.

"Why?" I asked.

"They won't miss me as much," he said, and my heart sank.

"I would. I can't let you do that. I can't do this without you," I blurted, and before I could hold the words in, I realized I had said it.

"It's already been decided. You owe it to your sister to be here. I, well, my only regret is that I have to leave you here. You deserve to never be abandoned again," he said, and I felt a sob starting to crawl up my throat.

"Guys, two things," Greg interrupted us, and we both jumped when we remembered he was sitting in the far corner. "One, I'm sure there's something that we can do. Two, I'm still here, and this sounds like a private moment. So before anyone says anything else, *remember*, I am a bad liar."

"What does that have to do with anything?" I asked.

"You're a lawyer. All you do is lie." Josh scoffed.

"Very nice. Look, I'm just letting you know, if someone asks if there's something going on, I'm not going to be able to confidently deny it," Greg groaned before placing the ice pack back on his face.

"We're going to figure this out. If they can't, we will," I said, wanting to unpack what Greg said, but deciding to focus on the elephant in the room.

"Rachel, I don't know. I don't know what to do, but I don't think we should make it worse," Josh shook his head.

"Josh."

"Rachel, promise me," Josh begged, putting his hands on my shoulders.

"Okay, fine," I sighed.

Chapter 16

Josh

Time didn't seem to exist the rest of the day. At times, I felt like hours had passed, though it had only been a few minutes, but then other times, minutes that passed were actually hours. Everyone seemed stressed. My body was so tired, but for some reason, I couldn't sleep. I figured it was anxiety about the inevitable. I was happy that no one tried to find me as I stayed locked up in my room. My phone remained on silent, despite the texts from Nina, who I knew I was supposed to game with that day. Nothing seemed to matter anymore. Plus, my social battery was negative.

It was night before someone decided that I'd had enough peace and knocked on my door. I opened it. Jason. Of course. He had changed into pajamas– it must have gotten pretty late. I guess time flew when you were having an existential crisis about being the reason why everyone you cared about was in danger. That's how the saying goes, right?

"Hey, I wanted to check up on you. Caesar was surprised you didn't come down to eat," he said.

"I'm not hungry. I had a snack when Greg got here," I replied.

"That was like twelve hours ago, dude," he said.

"Jason, I don't feel like talking to anyone right now," I mumbled.

"Sorry, I just wanted to check in. Also, maybe, ask you a question," he inquired nervously.

"Go ahead," I said, taking a swig of water from the bottle on my nightstand.

"Did you bang Rachel?" he asked, and I started to sputter.

"What? No! Why would you ask me that?" I asked.

"Because, you seem like you're all… *in love* with her," he said.

"So why would you ask me if I slept with her? You can be in love with someone you've never slept with. Look at your obsession with Nicole," I said, motioning to him.

"Thanks for reminding me of my failures and shortcomings, brother," he groaned.

"Sorry, I was making a point." I chuckled.

"Anyway, it just seems like you guys are into each other, and since you two have been here mainly by yourselves for over a month, I was just curious." Jason shrugged.

"Nothing happened," I said.

"And even if it did, I get it. She's beautiful, she's a dancer, she's funny… Just make sure you don't piss Nicole and Noah off. They probably wouldn't like that very much," he said.

"Jason, I'm not doing anything with her," I reminded him.

"Okay, but *if* you do…" He trailed off, flashing his eyebrows with a small smirk, which told me he did not really take what I had just said very seriously.

"Alright. Anything else?"

"Nope," Jason said before he slowly left my room with an entertained expression.

I woke up to Greg standing in my room, watching me intensely. He looked a thousand times better than he had the day before. His bruises had faded, he was in a clean suit, and he looked manicured once again. I gave him a tired nod of approval that he probably didn't care about on account of the face that he was giving me. I stared back at him, but he did not budge.

"Greg, how are you?" I asked dryly.

"I think I should be asking you the same thing." He snorted, crossing his arms.

"I am… taking it one day at a time," I said.

"Okay," he said with a curious smile.

"What? There's definitely something you want to know because it's only seven in the morning. You have way more things to worry about besides how I am when you already know the answer is not well," I said, sliding my glasses onto my face.

Greg slid his hands into his pockets, pacing back and forth across my room. I crossed my arms and watched him for a minute before I glanced at my phone. I had two texts. One was from Nina, and the other from Rachel.

Nina Perez: Hey, we were supposed to game the other day. Left me hanging. Call me.

Rachel Smith: Are you being harassed right now? Because at this point, fate by Tracey is looking good.

I was just about to respond to Rachel when Greg cleared his throat.

"Nothing you want to talk about?" he asked.

"Like what? My impending doom?" I asked.

"No, what's going on between you and Rachel?"

"We're both traumatized, if that's what you mean."

He ignored that. "So, nothing is going on? You two aren't an item?"

"No," I sighed.

He stared at me again. His eyes searched mine as if they would reveal some answer I wasn't already giving. He opened his mouth to say something, but a knock came from the door.

"Come in," I called.

Rachel walked in and crossed her arms. She nodded at Greg before looking over at me.

"We need to speak, alone," she announced.

"I'll leave you kids to it. I have some research to do anyway," Greg said.

"Please tell me that this research has to do with keeping us alive?" Rachel raised an eyebrow.

"Yes, hopefully," Greg agreed, before leaving the room.

Rachel turned back to me with an exasperated look. I gave her a tired sigh.

"So, number one, your brother is weird," she started.

"Which one?" I asked, even though I had a feeling I knew who she was talking about.

"Both, but this time I mean Jason," she said.

A knot formed in my stomach. The man did not know how to keep his mouth shut or when to stop. We needed to have a discussion on limits.

"He was asking me if I had a crush on anyone in the house, and I told him that he should fuck off if he doesn't want my fist to crush his face," she warned.

"Noted, I will make sure to relay the message." I chuckled to hide my annoyance.

"Actually, Noah was being weird this morning too, but that's a fact I've known for some years now. I guess you can't choose your brother-in-law," she sighed.

"What did he do?" I asked.

"He just stared at me and gave no explanation as to why," she said.

"That's weird," I grimaced.

"Right? Anyway, the reason why I'm here at this lovely hour is because I have some info on Tracey. I think we should stop her before the month is even up," she said.

"Stop her, how?"

"I don't know *yet*," Rachel said, matching my tone.

"That's not very helpful," I replied shortly.

"Okay, Joshy, what's your plan? Wait until she chooses who should die? I don't know about you, but I would like some more years before I tell the world deuces," she said.

"Ray, listen… A lot of things would have not happened if it weren't for my existence," I said.

"A lot of things also wouldn't have happened if it weren't for Noah's existence too. Do you see him standing in front of a fucking gun? No! Get it together because we need you. I need you."

I just stared at her. I wanted to cry. I wanted to cry for so many reasons, but I didn't. She groaned, exasperated, before she left my room with a slam of my door. I sank back onto my bed and let the feeling of hopelessness flow from my eyes.

Chapter 17

Rachel

Eliza was the one who had told me about Tracey and her whereabouts. She frequently listened in on her father's conversations with Tracey, just to be more in the know than not be. It was interesting how she never seemed to be afraid, just very matter-of-fact. Not like how I pretended to be, but actually nonchalant about everything that was happening to her. I wondered if life had just made her numb to it all.

Later that same day, I went to find her in Soteria. I looked everywhere, but she was nowhere to be found. I finally gave in and asked Noah, who was sitting in his office reading something with his classic scowl.

"Hey Crawford, where's Eliza?" I asked, making him slowly look up at me.

"Eliza? She's at school. She said she would be back tomorrow when classes are done for the week," he said.

"Ugh, fine, thanks," I grunted, about to leave.

"I'm surprised," he added with a small smile creeping up his lips.

"Surprised about what?" I asked.

"That you are looking for Eliza. You guys almost got into a fight a little over a year ago." He snorted.

"Noah, please, that was so two years ago," I said, leaning against the doorframe.

"Love to see the growth. Anyway, she has mainly morning classes, so if you call her she'll probably answer," he hinted.

"Thanks… Actually, Noah?" I turned back around to face him.

"Yeah?" He took a swig of whatever brown liquid was in his crystal glass.

"You trust Eliza, right? Like with your life?" I asked.

"Yeah, with my life," he said without blinking. "Why?"

"Because she's my best friend. She's gone through so much for me, and… I don't know. We have this unspoken agreement that no matter what, we have each other's backs," he explained, and his eyes revealed something really sad for a moment.

"Well, now it's spoken I guess," I said, trying to lighten the mood.

Noah's eyes rolled up to the ceiling and then back down at me with a smirk. If Noah had nothing else going for him, at least he was smart enough to find entertainment in my jokes. I thanked him again and headed up to my bedroom.

Upstairs, I locked the door and went into the bathroom to make sure no one could hear me through the door leading to the hallway. Then I called Eliza. She didn't answer when I called, but called me back within a couple minutes.

"Hey, Little Smith," she answered with a bored sigh.

"I need your help figuring out this Tracey situation," I said.

"I told you that she's probably hiding out somewhere in Jersey. That's all I know from eavesdropping on my dad's conversation with her a couple weeks ago," she said.

"Is there a way we can find out more? I want to take care of this problem before it takes care of me."

There was silence on the other end of the phone for a moment or two. I knew that Eliza knew what I was trying to imply–I just needed to know if she was in or not.

"You know that chasing the beast could lead to you being killed, right? Tracey's no joke," Eliza remarked.

"I'm tired of being tortured, Eliza. I can't continue to live like this. I don't think my brain can handle it anymore, and I'm most certainly not going to let Josh give himself up just so it can stop."

"Okay, let's talk when I make it back up to you tomorrow. Don't do anything until I'm there," she said.

"Alright, thanks."

Josh and I sat in silence in the kitchen as I finished my assignments due that day. I typed away on my laptop as Josh typed on his. I felt his eyes glance up at me from time-to-time, but he didn't say anything. Once I was done, I looked up at him and waited for his eyes to catch mine. After a minute or so, they did, and we just stared for a while. There was something so intoxicating about him, not like a drug, but a piece of art that was so well crafted, you had to stop and appreciate it each time.

"What?" he asked.

"You started it." I snorted.

"*Yes*, I did," he said.

"And that's because?" I asked.

"You've barely said anything to me since yesterday. I mean, I know everything has been a lot lately, but still."

"Joshy, since when did you think the world revolved around you? You know I have school," I teased.

"And yet, that has never stopped you from bugging me before," he said in the same teasing tone.

"Right, but things were different then," I said.

"Hmm, just doesn't seem right to me."

"Well, *newsflash Joshy*, I don't follow a rhyme or reason. I'm quite ungovernable, actually."

Josh's irritation flashed across his face, and in one swift move, he took my laptop. He held it up in the air, and there was no way I would be able to get it unless I got on the island, so that's exactly what I did. I swung my arms trying to get it, but he held it away from me again. I almost slipped, but Josh wrapped his other arm around my thighs to stabilize me. I got down on my knees and tried to reach my laptop, but it was up high again.

"You're so annoying!" I laughed.

"Thanks, that's my job." He smiled.

"May I please have it back now?" I asked, pouting and using my most convincing puppy-eyed look.

"Hmm…" He pretended to think about it. "No."

"Why not?"

"You have to promise to stop closing me out," he said.

"I'll think about it," I replied.

"Then no." He laughed.

He started to back up to make a run for it, but I grabbed a handful of his shirt. In another swift move, he was out of his shirt and running shirtless around the kitchen. His glasses were gone too. I slid to the other side of the island and jumped on his back. He finally fell, holding my laptop close to his chest like it was a baby. I turned him over and pried it out of his arms. He let it go as he breathlessly looked up at me, clearly entertained.

"Are you a dancer or a football player?" he asked in between breaths.

"Woah," a voice sounded before I could respond.

Josh and I looked up. Eliza and Noah stood in the foyer, staring at us through the entrance of the kitchen. At first, their stares were just emotionless. I realized the scene they were witnessing: I was straddling a shirtless, and let's be honest, very muscular, Josh. He gave me a wide-eyed, alarmed look before I stood up and gave him some space. Then I think we both realized that there was this sharp silence in the room, and I mean sharp enough to divide the country. We both started speaking at once.

"Hey guys, uh," Josh started.

"He took my laptop and–" I started.

"Yeah, we were just fooling around and–" he began.

"I bet," Eliza snorted with a smirk.

"Okay, enough, let's go, Eliza," I said, walking toward her and grabbing onto her arm to lead her upstairs.

"I wasn't done looking at him yet!" Eliza whined as she dragged behind me.

I heard Noah give a disapproving grunt at that as she and I walked upstairs. Before he was out of sight, I saw Josh watching me sheepishly

When we made it to my room, I locked the door behind us. Eliza had an unreadable expression on her face before she sighed and sat at the foot of my bed. The silence was beyond awkward, and I felt the need to fill it.

"Okay, so about Tracey… I'm thinking we could find a way to find out more information from your dad," I began.

Eliza put up her hand and started laughing. It wasn't often she showed so much emotion at once, and it made me pause.

"What?" I sighed.

"Okay, I know that this is serious and everything, but we're not going to talk about you and Josh downstairs just now?" Eliza laughed.

"There's nothing to talk about. I just wanted to get my laptop back."

"There is nothing to talk about? There is so much to unpack here!"

"Like what?"

"First off, Josh is willing to die for you. Next, he's hot. Did you see him? Do you see the way he looks at you?"

"He *does not* look at me in any way." I rolled my eyes.

"I know you did not just lie to my face like that," Eliza deadpanned.

"I'm being so serious." I chuckled.

"I'm just letting you know that he's into you," Eliza concluded.

"Anyway, what about Tracey?" I changed the topic.

"There is a way to find out more information," Eliza said uneasily. "My parents are holding a party at our house next weekend, maybe I can get into his office while he's distracted."

"Great, so let me know how that goes," I said.

"Um, you're going to come with me," Eliza said. .

"Why would I be at your parents' house? Why do we have to wait until the party?" I asked.

"He'll be distracted at the party, and you can make sure he stays that way. I'm barely home these days, so the party will be our chance." She shrugged.

"I don't know, Eliza. I haven't been around people much since everything happened. I haven't even been around my friends. Plus, why wouldn't you keep your dad distracted instead? You want my currently socially inept ass to keep him distracted?"

Eliza tilted her head sympathetically and came over to me. She put both my hands on my shoulders. The gesture reminded me of Nicole in a way.

"In all seriousness, do you think you can handle it? In this world, it seems like no one takes the time to ask shit like that," she said with what sounded like genuine concern.

"I really don't know, but I'm not giving myself a choice," I murmured after a few beats.

"I would have you go to his office, but honestly, the maid would ask why you're in that part of the house. Also, Dad barely speaks to me." She snorted.

"Why?" I asked curiously.

"That's a really long story that I'm not in the mood to tell."

Chapter 18

Rachel

The night before the party, I couldn't sleep. I had so much weight on my chest. It was almost like the stress you felt when you knew you had no business sleeping when you hadn't completed an assignment due the next day. It felt like the stress you felt when you would find out important news the next day–news that would change your life. I finally gave up on sleeping and went to Noah's kitchen. I had asked to stay at his apartment because I wanted to see Ang and Ash. It wasn't completely a lie! I mean, I did want to see them, but I think my brain also wanted to avoid people who would definitely remind me that my parents were dead at all costs. It's not like they would do it on purpose, but I knew they would do something to show me that they felt bad, and that, in the end, would remind me that my life was shit.

I sat down in the kitchen and looked out at the illuminated city in the distance. The view was beautiful, but I kind of missed the trees and stars that I would see at Soteria. My mind wandered to what Josh was up to. If he was up playing games, or reading, or if he had actually gone to bed early. Did I cross his mind as much as he crossed mine?

The fancy cappuccino machine started to hiss as it poured brown liquid into a large glass mug on the counter. When the sound stopped, I turned around to grab the coffee and screamed. Nicole leaned against the counter in a silver silk robe and a matching bonnet with her arms crossed.

"Why are you drinking coffee at four in the morning?" she asked after a yawn.

"Why are you awake judging my beverage choices at four in the morning?" I asked.

"I hear something going on at this hour, I'm going to see what's going on," she pointed out as she placed something on the counter with a clang. I took a closer look and realized it was a small gun. My jaw probably hit the shiny floor.

"Um excuse me, but what the fuck is that?" I asked.

"It's a pistol," she deadpanned, and I gave her an exasperated look.

"Okay yes, I can see that. Since when do you have one?" I asked.

"Since the probability of my life or someone that I love being in danger tripled," she said.

"How do you know how to use it?"

"Noah and I learned. Just in case."

"Have you had to use it?"

"No, not yet," she said.

We settled into silence, both silently understanding that this entire situation had taken a huge toll on the both of us. When my cappuccino finished brewing, I gave her a nod, grabbing the mug handle and turning back to the lights.

***

Mom and Dad went on about hospital politics as Nicole and I sat quietly and listened at the table. It had been a couple months since the trial, and Nicole was doing better, but that didn't mean much since she was hanging on for dear life before. She had to take medicine on her really bad days, but it made her different.

"And how about you, Nicole? How was school today?" Dad asked.

Nicole slowly looked up from her plate, bags beneath her eyes. We all knew the answer to that. School had just started without Noah, and everyone thought she had dated a murderer so the days had been going terribly, obviously. Medical degrees, and my parents still seemed to miss the mark with how to deal with this.

"It was okay, I guess," Nicole answered.

Mom and Dad exchanged a concerned glance that parents give that doesn't help anything. Nicole could see it, and I knew she felt bad, but she was just trying to make it through the day.

"At least your day was okay. Mine was absolutely chaotic. Whoever decided that eight periods a day was not too long for the growing minds of the youth was on crack," I said, lightening the mood.

Mom and Dad chuckled. Nicole smiled a little, and I was so happy to see her smile. It's not like I didn't actually think that, but realizing being slightly obnoxious would keep the unwanted spotlight off of her, and I soon found it being part of who I was.

"You just came back from summer break," Mom said.

"And I realized that I no longer want to be bound by the shackles of Jefferson High," I said.

Nicole thanked me with wide eyes and a smirk, and I wagged my eyebrows at her. I knew that, when she could, she would save me from whatever I needed saving from.

***

I told Nicole and Noah that "one of my friends" was coming to pick me up, and they didn't even question it. They were trying to play mom and dad, and they missed out on a key opportunity. *Amateurs.* I took the elevator down and met Eliza in a sleek red convertible that looked like it cost the same as four years of my college tuition. I heard its door unlock when I got close, and the butterfly door opened. I sat down in the plush, expensive leather seats. Before I could say anything, we were off.

"Nice car," I said, inspecting all the details.

"Thanks, it was a birthday gift from a couple years ago. You know, before my parents hated me," she said dryly.

"Because of shooting Tracey?" I asked.

"No, but I'm sure that didn't help," she sighed but didn't elaborate, and I was afraid to ask more.

When we got to Eliza's house, I tried my best to not gawk at the size of it. Pillars guarded the house past the four large steps that led to them. Eliza typed on a small keypad–how it could possibly open a door so big was a mystery to me, but it did. Through the doorway, a huge crystal chandelier hung from above, dimly illuminating the foyer. I followed her up the stairs to the second floor, and we took a long walk to her bedroom in silence.

Inside revealed a room that was fit for a princess, or, in this case, the heir to millions. Nicole and I hadn't grown up in poverty at all, but this was just on a whole other level. Eliza walked around nonchalantly, not even aware of what she had.

"Okay, so I have three dresses for you to choose from," she explained, pointing to three dresses that hung up on a rack against the wall that shined like pearls. I'd already decided that the red one was the best one there as soon as I walked into the room.

"The red one," I decided. What's our game plan?"

"It's pretty easy. You're looking to *spark conversation* with my dad and make sure he doesn't go to his office," she said.

"Okay, got it. And you sure no one isn't going to question why I'm here?" I asked.

"No, you're my guest. I can be friends with my friend's sister-in-law." She shrugged as she flipped her auburn hair in the mirror.

At the party, I wore my hair blown out and big. The red dress fit me tighter than Eliza probably assumed that it would, but it showed off my curves. It felt weird wearing something so tight, since I had been wearing mainly sweats for the past three months. I felt a few gross old men eye me, but I acted as if I were completely comfortable in the situation as I walked over to the waiter who held a tray of champagne flutes. I took a glass and tried to look casual, taking a sip and scanning the room for Daniel. It didn't take long to find a tall white man with a bald head in a sea of about fifty people.

Slowly, I made my way over to him. Eliza was speaking to him, and her eyes cut over to me for a moment before her dad could notice. I stayed far enough to not be seen, but of course being a sister in red probably was not the way to achieve that, so within seconds, he noticed me. Eliza gave me a tight smile, and I walked over.

"Dad, this is Rachel Smith. Rachel, this is my dad, Daniel," she introduced us calmly.

"Smith… You must be Nicole's sister," he concluded with a forced smile.

"Yes, I am. Nice to meet you, Daniel," I smiled, instead of calling him Mr. Craig.

"Likewise, Rachel," he said.

"How are things going for the company?" I asked, attempting to sound genuinely interested.

He gave me a thoughtful look before he spoke again. It was clear he was deciding on what he wanted me to know. His face seemed so familiar, and I realized it was because Eliza shared some of his features. I expected to be more afraid of him, but instead, he seemed pretty approachable. I wondered if he had done some of the horrible things Tracey had done. I mean, until about a year ago, they were business partners.

"It's going well. We're deciding to expand our technology department. I'm not sure if you heard that from mister and misses Crawford," he said.

It took me a long minute to realize who he was speaking about. I had never even thought about the fact that people probably referred to them as that. It sounded like a middle-aged couple, but neither were old enough to drink, legally at least. Noah told me that he had gone to rehab when he was gone. It wasn't for drinking, apparently. Some nights he downed that shit like it was water. I guess that was a side effect of the job. It also dawned upon me that Noah and Nicole almost never spoke about work unless we asked, so I had no clue what was going on with CCTV, besides the fact that it existed.

"No, they didn't mention it. That's really exciting. I'm curious as to what incited you guys to go in that direction." I could not have given less of a shit, but I wanted to give Eliza a head start before he started to scan the room for her.

"Well, Rachel, you're young. You know that tech is our future. We just wanted to make sure we were doing everything we could to stay up to date on what's new out there," he said.

"That's really great. I'm actually working on my degree in computer science," I remarked.

"Well, good luck with your future endeavors. Excuse me," he excused himself with a nod, shifting his focus to a man who was walking past us. I turned around to see who it was, and I saw his polka-dot bowtie. It was the Mr. Elliot Eliza had mentioned.

I followed Daniel with some distance between him and myself. With all the chatter it was a little harder, but I was still able to make out most of the conversation.

"Yes, I got the report. I have to take a look on Monday," Daniel said.

"Greg made some last minute edits that Crawford put in after the meeting. Any word on when his brother will be making his appearance?" Mr. Elliot asked.

"Next week, apparently. Do we have a location on TC?" Daniel asked in a hush tone, and, after a second, I realized that was Tracey's initials.

"We got a location somewhere in Edison. It's not clear where, exactly. I sent some details in the report. Crawford wants an exact location, but–" Mr. Elliot started.

"Let's delay things and wait until things have calmed down. We don't want to upset the apologists. There is a new deal with Senator Kaplan that's getting secured next week," Daniel said.

Mr. Elliot caught sight of me being close by and moved farther away. This time, I did not follow. Hopefully Eliza could get the details in that report. I was about to take a look at my phone to see if she had sent me any updates when I noticed everyone glancing in my direction. The light, boring music was still playing, and the chatter continued, but the attention was felt.

I turned around to see Josh standing there in a suit that was tailored to fit him perfectly. Even in heels, he still towered over me. His hands were in his pocket as he gave me a curious once over. A shadow of a smile appeared on his lips.

"Hey, Ray," he said.

Chapter 19

Josh

I was distracted, and for many reasons. First, from the moment I entered the room, I'd been receiving strange looks from many people. Women, that I'm sure were older than my mother, were giving me the eye. Then, a bunch of guys looked at me as if they were assessing whether or not I deserved to be in the room with them. Another reason I was distracted was because I was confused on why this party was so dull–I get that the average person here was just about triple my age, but still. I had barely been to any parties, and I knew this vibe was deplorable. The final reason, and the most distracting of them all, was Rachel's dress. She looked beautiful. Actually, she looked more than beautiful, she looked hot. I had no previous data on how to react so I just stared at her until I was noticed.

"Hey, Ray," I said, willing my eyes to remain on Rachel's face instead of wandering elsewhere. Trust me, it was easier said than done.

"Josh? What are you doing here?" Rachel asked.

"I was invited," I replied, nonchalantly.

"You were what? So if you were invited then that means that–" Eliza began, walking up behind Rachel.

"Rachel Lauryn Smith, what the hell are you doing here?" Nicole's voice asked behind me.

"Oh great, it's a fucking reunion," Eliza groaned, before throwing her champagne back in one swig.

"Eliza, why is Rachel here?" Noah asked, slowly walking up behind Nicole.

"I wanted to get out." Rachel shrugged casually.

"And you chose a benefit? Really?" Nicole asked dryly as if she were disappointed by Rachel's answer .

Noah cleared his throat extra loud, which made us all turn to him. I hoped he hadn't caught me looking at Rachel as she was turned around, but his eyes gave me an icy glare to tell me he had. His expression softened a bit when he made eye contact with Eliza. They exchanged a silent glance, and she looked away with a roll of her eyes.

"Anyway, since we're all here, why not make the best of it?" Rachel said cheerfully to lighten the mood. It did not seem to work, but she tried her best.

"Excuse me! Your hair just looks so curious. Can I touch it?" A frail lady with lipstick that was not her shade, but with pearls that made up for it, called as she approached Rachel slowly with her hand out. There was a younger woman behind her who looked like her daughter.

She was smiling like she wasn't young enough to realize this was socially not okay.

"Um, no," Rachel said, taking a step back.

"Oh, I just want to take a quick look," she replied.

"That requires your eyes, not your hands, ma'am," I said, taking a step in between Rachel and the lady. The lady glared at me, but I was not scared. My brother did that at least three times a day.

"Well if she doesn't want people to touch it then maybe she should actually get it done," the younger lady snapped before walking away with the older lady.

"Actually, bi–" Nicole started, but Noah put his arm around her.

"*Okay*, let's go to the basement," Eliza interjected.

The basement looked as if it were a normal level in the house. There was a corner resembling a wine cellar, closed off with a clear glass door. A bar counter was right next to it. There was a room housing a TV screen at least eighty inches in size, along with plush chairs for watching movies. Then, there was a living area with a gorgeous pool table and a huge sectional couch that could sit at least twelve people. Soteria was gorgeous, but this was on a different level.

Eliza walked into the cellar and grabbed a bottle of wine. She grabbed five glasses from behind the counter and poured the wine into them. She handed them out, and we all took one. It only took a minute for Rachel to notice that I did not take a sip.

"You don't like wine?" she asked before she tasted the wine in her glass.

"No, not really. Alcohol kind of tastes like poison," I admitted.

"What? How could you not like wine?" she asked, shocked.

"You asked the question, which means you knew there was a possibility that I, in fact, would not like wine," I said.

"Don't start throwing your logic to me in that tone," she admonished, giving me an incredulous stare.

I chuckled and turned my attention to see what everyone else was doing. Eliza held her wine glass by the base on one hand and was typing on her phone with the other. Music had started to play, and Nicole and Noah danced. She threw her arms around his neck and swayed to the music. He dipped her and pulled her back for a kiss. I caught Eliza gazing at them. She had put her phone down and watched with so many different emotions playing on her face at once.

"Wow, guys. This could be the champagne and wine talking, but I want a boyfriend," Rachel shared all on her own, but the wine definitely assisted.

"I just want the amount of serotonin those two have," Eliza replied.

"Yeah," Rachel agreed, longingly.

"I thought you hated men," I teased, lightly nudging her with my elbow.

Rachel sighed loudly, and I felt a smirk form on my lips. She rolled her eyes before she downed the rest of the wine in her glass. She closed her eyes for a long moment, savoring it.

"That good, huh?" I asked.

"I haven't had a drink in months," she hummed as she tapped the rim of the glass on her bottom lip.

I wanted to tease her about being under the age minimum for drinking, but instead, I stayed silent. I watched as she gazed at Noah and Nicole too. I couldn't read her eyes, and I wanted nothing more than to know what she was thinking.

"What's going on in your head?" I asked when Eliza slipped away from us.

"I know it's not true, but I always felt like she got it easy with this stuff. I mean, look at them. You can't tell me you've never looked at them and wished you had that too," she said softly so only I could hear. I let my eyes fall on Nicole and Noah again. It had been months since I heard both of them laugh the way they did.

"When I look at them, I see a king and queen in a castle that neither of them ever wanted… For as much as people envy them, I pity them. The amount of ___ they probably give up everyday that they will never tell us… just so we can be happy, to save us from the sorrow… I don't know. I'm glad they have moments like these. I think it keeps them alive," I replied.

I would forever be grateful to Nicole for being the sister I'd always wanted. I could talk to her about the stuff that Jason didn't have the touch for. I had Rachel too, but our relationship was so different. I didn't quite have a name for it, but it was different, and I couldn't imagine her not being there anymore either. That's why I had to be the one to go, not her. Rachel would survive without me, but I wasn't sure if I would be able to do the same if the tables were turned.

"Earth to Joshua Crawford," Rachel called as she snapped her fingers, breaking me from my train of thought.

I cleared my throat, bringing myself back into the moment. "Yeah?"

"Would you like to play pool?"

"Sure, but I don't know how to," I said.

"I'll teach you," she said confidently, and who was I to question it?

Chapter 20

Josh

I should have questioned it. It's not like it wasn't a spectacular situation to be in, but the spectacle of it all dimmed when I realized we still had an audience only twenty feet away. I began to feel on edge. The last thing I wanted was for someone to notice and say something stupid to make things awkward.

"So, you hold it like that. I mean, obviously I will not be here in your way, but your hands would be here, and you should lean in like how you are now," Rachel instructed, not realizing that she was killing me with a slow death as she pressed herself up against me to show me how to play.

"Okay," was all I could breathe out.

"Are you okay? Actually, you're right. Let's do a few practice shots," she said.

"Whatever you think is best," I mumbled, noticing how amazing she smelt.

"Alright, so you line it up, pull back and go forward. Try to go at the right angle or the ball hops, and you don't really want that. Unless you do... but let's just start with regular shots," she went on, and I took deep breaths as we practiced a few shots.

The stick hit the white ball, and the other balls dispersed with a satisfying click. None of them reached the holes. Rachel scanned the table thoughtfully. I watched her.

"Alright, let's try to make a shot, and then you'll go on your own," she said, but I really would have preferred if she stayed.

I nodded as we lined up. A perfect shot was made when a green ball with the number six on it plopped perfectly into one of the holes. She smiled and gave me a high five.

"Okay, I'm going to put chalk on my pool stick and then it's game on," she challenged.

I felt a presence behind me. Eliza stood there, smirking behind her glass. Even when she was entertained, her eyes appeared bored. I wondered if she and Noah had learned that from somewhere. Regardless, it made them mysterious.

"What?" I asked.

"You're poking out of your pants a little." She giggled.

"What?" I gasped, looking down. I wasn't.

"Just kidding," she said, amused.

"Why?"

"Because sources say you're *crushing* on her. It's cute," she said.

"Then you should get a refund from these sources. I'm not crushing on anyone," I lied.

"Oh please, pretty boy. I was not born yesterday." She scoffed.

"Alright, you ready?" Rachel asked, coming back from across the room.

"Are you, Josh?" Eliza asked with a smile before walking away.

Rachel gave me a confused expression after watching Eliza walk away.

"What was that about?" she asked.

"Couldn't tell you. You know how humans get when they are under the influence," I joked, and she simply rolled her eyes as a response.

That night, I slept on the couch. Rachel was in the guest room, and Nicole and Noah were in their room. I dreamt about pool.

The next morning, I woke up to movement. I opened my eyes, expecting a rush of light, but there was barely any light at all. I slid my glasses on and turned on a side table lamp to see Rachel dressed in black, a backpack strapped to her shoulders. She was almost at the elevator but froze in place when she heard me sit up on the couch.

"Where are you going?" I asked.

"Shut up," she whispered, "You're going to wake everyone."

"Waking everyone is the least of my worries. You're leaving the house at five in the morning," I criticized in a slightly lower volume.

She heaved an exasperated breath before quietly walking over to me.

"I am getting something done with Eliza, ok? I need you to act as if you don't know I'm not here," she ordered.

"How am I going to do that? What are you going to do?"

"Everyone is going to think I'm sleeping in until at least ten or eleven," she said.

"What are you going to do?" I asked.

"I can't tell you."

"Then I can't promise I won't tell."

She exhaled and threw her head back for a moment. I noticed how the glow of the lamp was playing on her skin. It looked so smooth. I wanted to touch it.

"Josh, I'm going to bargain with Tracey," she said.

"What? Bargain? Are you fucking crazy?" I asked, not realizing I cursed until it already happened.

"I need you to trust me. I got this," she hummed confidently.

"It's Tracey. No one *has* this. No one knows what she's going to do next," I argued.

"Do you trust me?" In the soft light, her eyes locked with mine, and I didn't have the power to look away.

"I trust you. I just don't trust her," I said gently.

"I promise, I'll be okay," she said, slowly backing away.

I pressed my lips together, a heavy knot forming in my stomach.

"I don't like this, Ray."

"But you like me, so at least there's that." She gave a cheeky smile over her shoulder, pressing the button for the elevator.

I knew what she meant, but for a second, I thought she was talking about something else, something more. I sighed and shook my head.

"Be back before tonight," I begged.

"I'll do my best." She shrugged, and the elevator closed. She was gone.

I didn't really sleep for the rest of the morning. Only the occasional doze here and there. Noah and Nicole came out of their room after seven, casually unaware that there was anything beyond the usual going on. I pretended to lazily peer at my phone. At first, they didn't say anything to me, which I preferred, but that was very short lived.

"Morning." Nicole smiled, walking past me to walk to the balcony.

"Morning." I yawned, pretending to still be tired.

Noah and I slapped hands as he followed Nicole onto the balcony. I wondered how long it would be until the peace was over. I wondered if Rachel was okay, and how, even though this was dangerous, I wanted to be out wherever she was.

Me: Hey are you ok?

Rachel Smith: Yeah I'm fine. Can't talk.

Sighing, I turned off the screen. A nice shower seemed to be in order, so I went to the bathroom and contemplated life as I let the warm water hit my skin. Music played from my phone, and the melody mixed with the sound of the running water, creating a false sense of serenity.

All of a sudden, things felt off. The door swung open, and the knob slammed against the marble on the wall. I didn't move at first.

"Josh," Noah shouted over the music and water.

"Yeah?" I responded.

"We can't find Rachel," he said, breathless.

"What? Did she go out?" I asked, so grateful I didn't have to show my face.

"Ah, maybe, but she knows it's not safe to go out without telling anyone."

"She's not answering her phone?" I asked.

"No. Do you know where she is?"

"No." I felt terrible for lying.

He didn't say anything for a moment, and I almost thought he left. Then I saw his silhouette through the glass. He had gotten closer. I felt a knot in my stomach.

"Josh, do you know where she is?" His tone shifted, like he already knew the answer.

"No, I do not. I've been here in the shower. I thought she was sleeping and wanted to get my shower in before she woke up," I responded evenly. "I'll be out in a minute, and we'll figure this out."

He was silent again. His shadow disappeared a bit. I allowed myself to breathe again.

"Fine. I'm going to make some phone calls," he grumbled, and I heard the door close.

When I got into the living area, Nicole was typing feverishly on her phone. Next to her was a glass mug of barely drunken tea. When she noticed me, there she gave me a blank stare, one that you had when there were too many emotions happening on the inside to show on the outside. I walked over and put an arm around her.

"She'll be okay, Nicole," I promised.

"There's three million missing," she responded, and my eyebrows went up.

"Three million, *what?*" I gaped.

"Toe nails. Obviously, dollars, Josh," she sighed, stress lining her voice. I wanted to laugh, despite everything. I was worried out of mind about Rachel too, but I felt a smirk start to crawl up my face nonetheless.

Nicole peered up from her phone. She was giving me an expression that I could not read, and I won't lie to you, I was a little frightened by it. I got why Noah was scared of her sometimes. She was small, but I'm sure she could move boulders if you got her started.

"Are you laughing right now?" Her lips formed a firm line.

"No, I'm not. I might be, but… okay three million dollars," I said, changing the topic. "Where did she even get that?"

"Our parents left us some money, and then we got the returns from the life insurance policies. Noah and I also put some money in the joint account I have with her. I told her to use what she needs, but I didn't expect three million to be missing. Did she mention anything to you?" Nicole asked.

I froze for a moment, starting to feel uncomfortable. *Why would she assume that there was a possibility that I knew anything?* Realizing that more time than socially acceptable passed, I tried to seem like I was deep in thought.

"I don't think so," I said, rubbing my chin.

"You sure about that?" Noah's cold tone made me jump as he walked into the kitchen.

"Yeah, why would she tell me?" I asked.

"Because you two are close." Nicole shrugged, bringing her phone to her ear and excusing herself to make a phone call.

Noah began to say something, but I was saved from an impending lecture by the ping of the elevator. Within seconds, Greg emerged through its doors, and he wasn't dressed in a suit. Instead, he had on all gray athleisure. His hair was wet, and he was out of breath. It was weird seeing him like that. It wasn't the first time I had seen him out of his usual clothes, but it happened so infrequently that I felt like I had to stare for a second.

"We need to get in the car *now*," he said, the urgency in his voice made my skin prickle.

"Why, what happened?" Noah asked.

"Rachel and Eliza are in New Jersey," he replied.

"Okay, and why is Jersey important? What's there besides bad drivers?" Noah urged.

"Your mother and her clan, smartass," Greg snapped at him.

"Fuck," Noah breathed as he ran to get Nicole down the hall.

Greg typed on his screen, and then stopped before he glanced up at me. He looked at me pointedly.

"You knew about this," he accused, low enough so only I could hear.

"Me? No, I didn't," I said, forcing my face to remain impassive.

"Whatever." He ran a hand through his hair. "Tracey does not play by the rules. We need to get them out of there before there's any more surprise accidents. I don't think this group can handle any more of those."

Jason met us at Soteria. Greg said that anyone involved needed to be safe and not be in the way while he figured out how to get Rachel and Eliza out of whatever mess they were in. It was spring break, and Jason did not seem pleased with being bothered.

"Why are they in Jersey?" Jason asked again as we all sat around the kitchen island.

"You know, Westbrook, the answer is not going to appear out of thin air because you keep asking it," Noah grumbled.

"No, but *what's* in Jersey? Someone definitely knows something. I'm not asking you guys to be psychic but give me something," he pleaded.

"My mother is in Jersey," Noah said.

Jason leaned back in his seat and scratched the shadow that was growing in on his face. He glanced over at me for a second before he looked back at Noah.

"Are they crazy?" He shook his head in disbelief.

"I'm hoping this makes sense soon," I said, ignoring the growing worry in the back of my mind.

"Are they far?" Jason asked.

"From what Greg said, they're about an hour away," Noah answered.

A loud noise blared in the distance. Noah's head shot up from his phone, and he raised an eyebrow. Then his eyes lit up in familiarity. Nicole put a hand on his arm to get his attention.

"I think it's one of our helicopters," he explained.

Nicole slid off her stool and went over to the front door. When she opened it, her curls blew to one side. Noah ran out after her and looked up at the helicopter that was now very close to the house. It sounded like it was nearly landing on the roof. Greg rushed through the door with Eliza in his arms. She was covered in dirt, her leg wrapped in bandages. Her face was scrunched up in pain, and Greg looked like he was doing his best not to make whatever happened to her worse. Rachel walked in behind them with someone from security. She was shaking, her mouth clamped shut. Noah nodded his head at the security guard and took over, standing next to Rachel.

"What happened? What's going on?" Noah asked.

Rachel turned to him with wide eyes and started to sob. Nicole ran up from behind them to her sister's other side. She wiped the tears off her face.

"What's going on?" Nicole asked, her voice hushed and calming.

Rachel focused on Greg as he examined Eliza's leg. Something felt so wrong.

"I'm so sorry, Noah. I didn't mean it," Rachel said in between sobs.

"What do you mean?" Noah asked with a touch of unease in his voice.

"Your Mom, she's gone," Rachel croaked.

Noah paused, a confused expression on his face. I found myself next to him with a hand on his back.

"What happened?" Nicole asked.

Chapter 21

Rachel

For the record, I never wanted this to happen. I never wanted Tracey Crawford dead. Okay, *actually*, I totally would've been cool with Tracey being dead. She had made all of our lives absolutely miserable. She didn't deserve to live happily outside the confines of a jail cell. I just didn't want to be the reason why she was gone. I never planned to be the reason why she was gone.

Our plan was simple. Tracey wanted two things—money and power. Power was not something I was in a position to give, but money... I had recently fallen into some of that. I wanted to negotiate with her. Three million dollars to make the bullshit go away. I thought it was a pretty solid plan. Evil people got paid off all the time, right? Eliza and I had done some digging, and we had found where Tracey was hiding out. It was a small log cabin in the middle of the woods somewhere in Jersey.

That morning, Eliza and I drove out before dawn. It was quiet for a while before we began to speak. It was still dark, and, besides the little peak of sun coming over the horizon, the only light in the tinted car was that of the dashboard.

"So when are you and Josh going to get it over with?" Eliza asked.

I almost spat out my coffee. "Excuse me?"

"You know, when is that going to happen?" she repeated.

"When is what going to happen, exactly?"

"Hooking up." She shrugged.

I turned to her slowly with a dropped jaw. She snorted, and I imagined her eye roll under her sunglasses. I gulped my coffee hard and cleared my throat.

"It is not like that at all," I said, laughing lightly.

"But you want it to be like that." It wasn't exactly a question—more a statement, like she knew something I didn't.

"Why do you think that?" I asked, very thrown off by the conversation.

"You two are, like, in love with each other and don't even know it. It's kind of cute."

"In love? Why would I be in love with Josh? You've met him right?" I snorted.

"I have, and he's godly. He's really sweet and smart, and he's really pretty to look at," she went on.

"Then why don't you date him? He's closer to your age anyway," I said, sounding way more defensive than I wanted to.

"Because you're my friend. You would never get past that heartbreak, even if you don't know it yet," she said.

I went quiet. It's not like the thought hadn't come up. It had become the topic of discussion a few times over the past few months. Josh was undeniably a great guy. He was so attentive and always had my back. He was willing to give up his life so I could live. There were a few problems though. Josh was part of my family through marriage. I'm sure there was something somewhere that said a relationship between in-laws should not be a thing.

Then, there was the fact that we were just different. He didn't look like me, and because of that, the world saw us differently. I, a dark-skinned woman, represented some of the things society hated. He, a biracial man, was still a black man at the end of the day, but it was different. People would treat him better like Taylor, just because he had caucasian features. How would he ever understand me?

It was not that I did not want him. If I am being completely honest with all of you, I really did want him. If anything, I wanted to know what it would be like to bring down that barrier and be with him just once, but then I'm not sure if the barrier would ever properly go back up. It probably wouldn't, and I didn't want to ruin what we had. There was no doubt that what we had was precious. Thing was, I wasn't quite sure what to call what we had.

"Besides, I don't think Josh could ever love me like he loves you. And that's okay. I'm not sure I like the nerd type anyway," Eliza continued, drawing me out of my train of thought.

"He doesn't love me," I laughed, shaking my head.

Eliza shook her head and chuckled to herself. She didn't say anything else, but it made me want to ask her about what she knew. Had Josh expressed this? Why hadn't he said anything? But she seemed to have no interest in going back and forth any further because she turned on the car's sound system and began to play music.

We soon found ourselves driving on a dirt road along towering trees. Eliza's speed had decreased by quite a bit, but we were still making good time. We finally stopped when I saw a small light in the distance up on a hill. Eliza slowed to a halt and quickly turned the car off. She got out of the car, brought a pair of binoculars to her face, and looked in the direction of what I was able to make out as a small cabin.

"Yeah, it's them," she confirmed.

"How do you know?" I asked.

"I just do," she said, and I could tell there was something more to it, but this was not the time to dwell on it.

I threw my duffle bag over my shoulder and climbed up the steep hill with Eliza next to me. Some time had passed, and now it was bright enough to see our way around. We tried our best to make as little noise as possible, but it was hard when everything else around us was so quiet. Actually, the quiet was deafening, and it made me feel on edge. I felt as if my heartbeat was too loud. When we got to the top, Eliza swung her backpack around to her chest and opened it. She pulled out a pistol and handed it to me like it was a piece of candy. I gaped at her.

"Excuse me, but what the fuck is this?" I whispered loudly.

"Just in case," she said, lifting a shoulder.

"Who do you think I am?" I asked, my eyebrows reaching my hairline.

"Look, none of that matters here. In this world, the *Smith Core Family Values,* or whatever the hell you and your sister abided by, don't count. No one has a soul, and you will be killed if you're not ready to kill that person first. This is just in case, but I will have your back," she pledged.

"Why are you so prepared for this stuff?" I asked.

"Because… this is all I know," she said, and there was so much pain in her voice.

"Well, thanks," I said. "So the plan is to get in there, offer her the money, sign the agreement, and get out of here. I guess we'll give ourselves thirty minutes."

Eliza nodded, and I led the way to the cabin. I knocked on the door, and soon enough, a man opened the door. He was tall with a scar cutting across his face. He narrowed his eyes at me, and then looked curiously at Eliza. He was about to shut the door, but I put my foot in the doorway to stop it.

"I need to speak to Tracey," I declared.

"She's not here," the man grunted.

"Miles, no funny business. We know she's in there," Eliza said, casually.

He stood back to reveal an empty cabin, but something didn't feel right. Someone else was around. The snap of a branch sounded from behind us. I whipped around. Two people were running a few yards from us. They were only shadows, but I could tell one was Tracey and the other was a man. A gun went off, and Miles was on the floor. I turned to Eliza, who was holding her gun up with one hand.

"What? Why did you shoot?" I asked, horrified.

"He was about to charge toward us. Move, let's go," she demanded, backing up quickly.

I followed her down the hill as fast as possible. We jumped in the car and followed the two shadows we saw running. The woods became too dense, forcing us to abandon the car and start running. It was a lot more rocky than it appeared, and I had to alternate between watching the shadows and keeping my eyes down to make sure I didn't fall. We caught up a lot closer to them, and that, with the combination of the increasing light, allowed me to see them clearly as they made their way to an old car. It sat in a clearing of the woods with a dirt road nearby.

"They have a car," I panted, before I started to increase my speed.

Eliza hollered It pierced the early morning air and caused me to freeze. Over my shoulder, she laid on the ground. It looked like she had tripped over a rock. I was about to go back for her, but she put her hand out to stop me.

"Keep going! Stop them," she cried.

It didn't make any sense. Not really. I mean, what exactly would be my plan if I could catch up to them?

I had no clue, but I kept running. Tracey and the other man ran into the car. I knew if they drove off, I would lose. Losing would mean either Josh or I died. I pulled the pistol out, and without thinking, I started shooting in the direction of the car. It started to race off, but I kept firing shots. I needed to flatten their tires.

That's when it happened. I steadied my shaking hands and fired one more shot. It looked like I finally hit a tire, but then all of a sudden, flames erupted from the car. The car kept going until it hit a tree. I watched, confused for a moment, until I realized what I had done. I just caused the car to explode. I did that. There were people dying in that car. And they were dying because of something I did. The thoughts began to sink in. The air left my lungs. I wasn't sure what to do. *Should I go to the car and try to save them? Should I call someone?* I rushed back to Eliza, who had propped herself up against a log. Her wide eyes stared at me as I approached. When I asked her if I should go over to the car, she told me not to. We didn't say anything else to each other as we processed what was going on not too far from us.

I sank down on the ground as tears welled up in my eyes. I was not sure what I wanted to happen, but it was not this. Eliza took some time to slide over to me but finally put an arm around me.

"It's okay," she murmured, but her face didn't show that she really believed everything was going to be okay.

"I didn't mean to," I sobbed.

"I know," she said softly.

Eliza pressed the button to power on her phone. It was time to get help. We couldn't do this ourselves. We tried to, and we failed. Her signal was weak and nothing was going through. We made our way back to Eliza's car, and it took what seemed like hours since we had to walk so slow. Eliza leaned on me, limping by my side. When the car was in sight, we heard the blades of a helicopter.

So now, there I was, an eighteen year old girl with blood on her hands. A killer. A murderer. A criminal. I wondered if anyone would ever look at me the same. Whenever they looked at me, would they just think of someone capable of murder? They probably didn't trust me, and honestly, I wasn't sure I trusted myself.

When I couldn't cry any longer, everyone wanted answers. Eliza was in the office, getting her leg checked out by a visiting nurse. Noah, Nicole, Jason, and Josh all sat around the living room, waiting for me to tell them the tale of the morning. And that is exactly what I did. I was in tears by the end. Looking at Noah was what did it for me. I knew he didn't have a great relationship with his mother, but I was sure this wasn't easy for him to hear.

"I'm sorry," I said to everyone, but mainly to him.

"It's not your fault," he answered in almost a whisper before walking off.

Nicole followed him out the room. She didn't look at me much, and I felt uneasy about what our conversation would be like when the time finally came for it to happen. I wondered if she would see me differently; as a murderer. Watching everyone else in the room, I wondered if they thought that too. The thought was embarrassing.

"Are you hurt?" Greg asked, emerging from the far corner of the room.

"No, maybe bruised, but I'm okay," I said with a small shrug.

Greg nodded, a small frown appearing on his concerned face, and went to check up on Eliza. That left me with Jason and Josh. Josh was staring off into space with a finger over his lip, while Jason watched me with a look I couldn't read.

"What?" I asked, even though I knew what. I had killed someone.

"Are you okay?" he asked.

"I just said that—" I began.

"No, are you okay on the inside? Like mentally. Because the broken arms and bruises–that stuff can heal after a few months, but the broken parts and bruises on the inside... Those are even more important, especially because that stuff doesn't heal as fast," he said.

It was probably the first time I was in agreement with Jason in the two years I had known him. The thing was, I wasn't sure how to answer him. I wasn't sure if I was okay. I had done something awful; one of the most awful things a human could ever do. I killed people. Now, from what I could remember, that was not my intent. But that didn't matter in this case, right? I committed murder. Shit, I was a murderer. I killed more than one person, and for that night, I was sure I was considered a serial killer until I looked it up later on.

"I don't know. I'll have to get back to you," I responded as I made eye contact with Josh, who had finally decided to venture out of his train of thought.

Jason glanced over his shoulder at him as he began to make his way over to me.

"I'll leave you two to talk," he said, and he was gone.

Josh and I stared at each other for a minute or two. There were so many things to be said, but also none at all.

"You're quiet," I said, breaking the silence.

"Dude… Ray… What have you done?" he asked.

That was not the response I was expecting. My mouth dropped open for a moment before I stood up and moved closer to his face. *What had I done?* I saved his life! That's what I had done.

"Listen, Joshua, you have no right to judge me. Especially when you were going to just let yourself get killed!" I exclaimed.

"So you went and killed people? Shit, I can't do this," he said, walking over and putting his forehead against the window.

"Can't do what, Josh? I couldn't let it end this way." A sob climbed up my throat.

"And now you have blood on your hands," he sighed.

He really didn't get it. He knew what happened, and he still didn't get it. I walked to my room as the tears flowed from my eyes. In his eyes, it wasn't the intent that mattered, but the results. I didn't think any reasoning would really matter to him. When you lived sheltered your whole life, how could you see beyond just right and wrong?

Chapter 22

Josh

I was in pain, and I couldn't find a way to make this stop. Getting shot would've felt better. The night of the incident, and for the following days, I found myself having (what felt like) an existential crisis. I knew Rachel had the right intentions, but I was just so angry at her. She could've died, and it was for *me*? It didn't make sense. She had done something that could never be undone. Even though it was partially done to help me, I felt betrayed.

My time of screaming into the void ended when it was time to finally face The Table. The day before, I was fitted into a really expensive suit, had my hair cut, and stubble trimmed immaculately. It felt like I was going to court.

"Why do we care about what they think if we don't even like them?" I asked as I watched Noah get his facial hair trimmed. He had a nice goatee growing in now. I remembered when he was clean shaven.

"Because as much power I have, they still have so much more. I don't want those judgemental assholes to nitpick anything," he said.

How stressful it must be to exist like that. Would I be able to? I wasn't so sure, but I guess I didn't really have a choice.

"So you walk on eggshells around them? And Nicole too?" I asked.

Noah glanced over at me with a raised eyebrow and a slight frown.

"Especially Nicole. She's a black woman that they don't want to be there. I know it's hard for her, but she doesn't bring it up too much anymore. I don't want to make her think about it more than she must, but I check in and make sure I don't have to kill anybody," he said casually.

I chucked and sighed, but he looked over at me again. He was so serious, it brought a chill to my skin. *Maybe facing Tracey would be better than whatever I'm going to walk into,* I thought.

"How are things between you and Rachel?" he asked after a few moments of silence.

The answer to that question was worth plenty in gold. I would pay crazy money to know because, at that point, I didn't.

"I don't know. We haven't spoken," I answered honestly.

Noah nodded in understanding as he paid the hairdresser. She quickly gathered her things before she headed to the elevator. When the doors closed and she was gone, Noah turned to me with a knowing, condescending, bored look. I wanted to roll my eyes.

"It's quite clear you're in love with her, so what's the problem now?"

"I don't know if I can get over what happened. I mean, can you?" I asked incredulously.

Noah looked down, walking over to the glass doors that showcased a beautiful cast of orange over the city. With all the light of the sunset, all I could see was his silhouette. I saw his shoulders rise and fall.

"I knew I wouldn't have her forever. Something was going to happen. She was just too destructive. I just thought I might've had more time," Noah admitted. "It's funny because even though I hated her, I still loved her too. Anyway, you need to speak to Rachel. She did this because she didn't want your life to be in danger. I respect that."

"So you don't hate her? She killed someone. That *someone* is your mother," I pointed out.

"No, I don't think I could ever hate her. She's so tough on the outside, and I think those people get overlooked. But she's so good. If I can say one thing about Rachel, it's that she always means well. It was a mistake.

She's such a good person, and she's hurting. You can't just leave her to go through all of this herself," he said, his back still to me.

"I don't know if I can handle this," I argued.

"Then you don't get to speak to her when things are good either. That's not how that works. If you're going to abandon her, then that's it. You're either in or out," he said, turning to me and giving me a glare that could kill a whole village at once.

"What?"

"Do you understand?"

I nodded, and that was it. He went into his room, leaving me alone. If Noah was nothing else, he was loyal.

The next morning, Noah, Nicole, and I rode in silence to the CCT building. I was really on edge—unable to even eat. I needed this to be over. We had prepared for this day, but still, it seemed like no one could truly be prepared for what could happen at these meetings.

We traveled down the hallway, and my heart beat so fast, I probably was close to cardiac arrest. Nicole placed a hand lightly on my back. She barely looked at me, but it was like she knew what I was feeling. Noah kept his attention straight forward with the scowl he usually wore like a piece of armor.

"We got your back, always," she promised, her voice soothing as we entered the dark room.

Inside, there was a long, dark wood table surrounded by dark colored walls. The walls appeared to be covered in velvet–very expensive. The low light and the texture created shadows and beyond the table seemed like a space that would swallow you whole. It appeared that just about twenty people stood around the table. Every single one of them watched me, assessing me. I don't think that many people had looked at me at once before that point. My stomach turned, and I wondered if that's what stage fright was like.

All I wanted was to *not* be there. Ahead of me, Noah reached for Nicole's hand. When he finally found it, his shoulders seemed to ease. My stomach knots morphed into pangs. It wasn't because I wasn't happy that they had each other to hold onto, but because the person whose hand I would have held onto right now probably felt so abandoned.

When we got to the other end of the room, I saw Mr. Craig. He nodded at me, and I nodded back. There was something that was so mysterious about him, like he knew something I didn't. Maybe it was just his appearance.

It was genetic–I mean, Eliza looked like that too, but something told me that he was someone that had a lot of answers to the questions we all had. That's probably why Noah kept him around.

"Alright, this meeting is officially in session. We have a couple bylaws we want to review, some funding requests, but most importantly, I have the honor of introducing my brother to all of you today, Joshua Crawford," Noah said, giving me a rare smile.

Everyone did a little golf clap, and I bowed my head in gratitude, even though I was ninety-eight percent sure I hated all of them to some degree. There was something that was so off-putting about them–I doubted any of them had a clue what real life was like. I mean, did I?

"Can't forget about your mother's murder," a man with bowtie interrupted loudly.

The room got eerily quiet, and Noah's eyes slowly slid over to him. The man's satisfied smirk instantly vanished. I had to hand it to my brother, he should get an Academy Award for his facial expressions. They always perfectly conveyed his disgust with humanity.

"Yes, we will discuss the matters of this past weekend," Noah said with a slight strain to his voice.

"So, are we going to hold your uncivilized, criminal sister-in-law accountable for the matters of what happened?" asked a man with an overly groomed mustache.

Noah sent a glance over his shoulder to Nicole. Nicole pressed her lips together, staring at the man with narrowed eyes. I felt my body temperature raise. Was he really speaking to them like this? Why didn't they seem surprised?

"Mr. Abbott, I sincerely appreciate your concern, but I do have a small request– make that an order, be mindful of the words you use to describe *my* sister, as *I* am the one who is making decisions on *your* funding request," Nicole warned. The tightness in her voice made everyone turn in his direction.

"Ms. Smith-Crawford, I just mean–" he began.

"I find it very interesting that my sister is *uncivilized*, as there are several people in this room who have had a hand in some deplorable happenings as well. They were not uncivilized, but she is," Nicole went on.

"Respect your elders, young lady," the man with the mustache snapped.

"And I suggest you remember your place, Mr. Abbott," she said, which made him sink in his seat. A couple of people smirked. It appeared not everyone disagreed with what Nicole said. I mean, even if they did, I don't think they would dare show it. She was terrifying and held no punches. It became glaringly obvious that she and her sister were cut from the same cloth.

The meeting continued, and Nicole and Noah spoke about different topics like fundraisers and elections. It was weird to see the things that happened in the world from this side. They really were running things that happened everyday in society. They clearly had so much power, and it was even more clear that none of it phased them anymore. Noah finally looked over at me, and I knew it was *my time to shine. Great.*

"The introduction and town hall will be taking place now," Noah announced.

I stood up, feeling like I was some science project on display. I had on a full suit, though I felt completely naked. I cleared my throat and began to speak, peering down at my notes.

"Good morning, everyone. Thank you for having me," I began and looked up. Everyone gave me their undivided attention.

I looked over at Nicole and Noah, and they both gave me supportive smiles. Mr. Craig watched me curiously from the back of the room. I noticed Greg standing in the corner with a relaxed smile plastered on his face. It was then I wished I had Rachel to look to. She would either give me an encouraging look or a funny face—either would help me relax. I didn't deserve either from her at that moment.

"Spending almost twenty years away from this life and what it entails gives me a different perspective on The Table and what it does. Similar to, I'm sure, what my sister-in-law felt when she first got married to my brother, I feel apprehensive. There has been both good and bad that has occurred here. Even though I am Carter Crawford's first born, I have no interest in taking over Noah's position. There is no one else I could see leading The Table to where it needs to be. I am here to observe and play smaller roles in supporting my brother the best way possible," I said.

"How old are you, Joshua?" A woman's voice inquired.

"I'm going to be twenty-two later this year," I responded.

"Carter's children all must have a role. Do you have any preferences on what that role would be?" A man with silver hair asked.

"Not yet," I replied.

"Are you married?" The woman with the friendly voice asked again.

"No," I shook my head.

"A young bachelor on the market. Daniel, the tabloids will love that," the woman chimed in with a grin.

Noah gave me a quick, exasperated look. I had searched him up in the past, having found a few articles about him being a young, rich bachelor. It was pretty cringe, and I would have to hack the articles off the internet somehow if anyone ever had the awful idea of doing that for me.

"What's your stance on what happened to Tracey? She wasn't your mother, but I'm sure you must have felt something," Mr. Abbott asked.

"Tracey was not a fan of mine and made that fact perfectly clear. I have no emotional ties to her, but I hope she rests in peace," I said.

"That didn't answer the question," the man next to him in the bowtie pushed.

"I think that wasn't the answer you wanted," I retorted.

"So you condone that female's thuggish behavior then?"

"*Thuggish?* We're using *that* word?" I gaped, and so did everyone else.

"I didn't intend for it to come out like that." Mr. Abbott chuckled nervously.

"Well, I've always been taught that people are held accountable for their actions, not their intentions, Mr. Abbott," I nodded, trying to keep my composure.

Mr. Abbott rolled his eyes, sighing in exasperation. It didn't sit well with me that they spoke about Rachel like that. I didn't want to imagine how bad it must have been when we weren't there.

"Does it matter how it came out? That girl killed a very important member of our society," he finally said.

"Her name is Rachel. What you fail to note, Mr. Abbott, is that Tracey was terrorizing Rachel, and myself, for weeks. She told us that she was going to kill one of us to make our families hurt. Rachel went to negotiate with her, and things got out of hand. I know that piece of information may mean nothing to you, but it does to me. What I see is a woman who tried to put an end to the violence and agony." My fingers gripped my notes until my knuckles began to throb.

The kind looking woman, who asked very simple questions before, raised a finger before she began to speak.

"Gentlemen, it seems like we're going to disagree across the board here. I think this is what Noah was trying to speak about last year. Why don't we put things in place so it doesn't have to come to this?" she asked, and I felt a touch of happiness that someone here was at least a little more moral than the rest.

"Thank you, Mrs. Spinelli. I say, considering the events that took place, we review some of my initiatives from last year," Noah nodded in appreciation.

Mrs. Spinelli gave me a friendly smile, and I nodded gratefully at her. She whispered something to her husband that made him smile, as well. I was very curious as to what it was.

When the meeting was adjourned, I stood near Noah and Nicole as they answered some private questions from various individuals. I felt a tap on my shoulder and turned around to see the woman who was apparently Mrs. Spinelli. She wore her hair a little past her shoulders, dressed in a navy blue dress and matching sweater. It looked like something the first lady would wear. Her smile was friendly as her eyes assessed my face.

"You look like them—I mean him," she faltered.

"Oh… Yeah," I said, noticing her error.

"Anyway, it's wonderful to meet you, Joshua. My husband and I look forward to working with you," she offered with a smile.

I nodded and joined her in a two-hand handshake that people do to be friendlier than just a regular handshake. She was gone, disappearing into the small sea of people. Mr. Craig walked up to me with a small smile.

"Josh or Joshua?" he asked, his tone much warmer than I expected.

"Josh is fine," I answered.

"Well, Josh, it's so great to finally meet you. It's always a pleasure to meet someone connected to Carter," he said.

"You were best friends, right?"

"Yes, we were like brothers." He gave a fond smile.

"Do you miss him? I do," I shared.

"Of course. It hasn't been the same since he left," he said softly.

"For sure," I agreed.

"Well, it was nice speaking to you Josh. Contact me anytime," he said, and he slipped away.

I looked over, watching Noah whisper something into Nicole's ear, making her laugh in response. Even in a stressful environment like the one where we stood, they still managed to look so happy. It made me think of Rachel.

***

It was day two of teach-Josh-how-to-drive week, and Rachel said she would take a crack at it. She had finally gotten home after a three week thing called a dance clinic, and I was just happy to see her, even though I did really want to learn how to drive. At this point, it was just embarrassing not knowing how at my age, and I didn't care that there was a seventy-five percent chance for rain. I was going to hold on to that twenty-five percent.

"Hey loser, you ready to learn how to drive?" Rachel asked as she got in the car.

She looked immaculate, and I realized I was staring at her. I didn't know why at first, though. So I just studied her in hopes of figuring it out. I noticed that she had cut her hair a little, which made her curls sit higher up. Her skin was even more bronzed by the sun, and she looked even more toned than she did before. Whatever dance clinic was, it seemed like a great idea to me.

"What?" she asked with a chuckle, referring to the probably goofy expression on my face.

"Nothing. You look nice," I said, clearing my throat.

"Oh, well thanks," she beamed.

I drove slowly around her neighborhood, listening intently as she gave me instructions. We had to stop when buckets of water fell from the sky. I drove even slower back to her house. I put the car into park, and when I looked over, I saw an uneasy look on Rachel's face.

"I don't have an umbrella," she groaned.

I glanced outside as heavy raindrops hit the windshield, making it hard to see. Even after a few minutes, it didn't seem like the rain was going to let up. I took off my jacket and opened my door.

"Josh, what are you doing?" Rachel asked, her mouth agape.

"I'm walking you to the door," I said.

"But you'll get wet," she called, but I closed the driver's door behind me anyway.

I put my jacket over my head and opened her door. She looked at me like I was crazy but got under the jacket anyway. We ran up the long pathway to her house, and when we reached the front door beneath a little covering, I let my jacket down. We were still quite wet. Rachel's curls were hanging low, heavy with water, and little droplets wandered down her face. Her clothes were pretty doused too. Really, my jacket did nothing to help.

"Look at us!" She chuckled as she swiped the water off her bare arms.

"I'm sorry. I tried," I said.

"That's okay. Water dries, right?" She smiled, looking to be on the edge of laughter.

"What's so funny?" I asked, a smile creeping over my lips.

"Your hair. I've never seen it wet before. You look funny." She snorted.

I examined the reflection in the glass of her door and saw my hair looked like I rolled out of bed and then spent thirty seconds in the shower. Some strands hugged my forehead–I *looked* weird. I don't know what possessed me to do it, but I shook my head really hard, spraying water from my hair onto her. She gasped loudly. She reached for me, and I grabbed her arms to stop her from throwing a few punches. At first we laughed, but that eased into us just gazing at each other. That was the first time I wanted to kiss Rachel Smith, but I didn't. I didn't because *what the hell was I thinking?* I was obviously hallucinating because there was no way she would want to kiss me back. Did I even want to kiss her? Yes. Was it illegal to try to kiss your sister-in-law's sister? Probably.

My mind was all over the place, and I ended up taking a couple steps back. Her expression was unreadable, until I realized she was probably judging me for letting my back get more wet in the rain.

"I should go," I announced.

"Okay," she said softly. I held her gaze for another second or two and walked back to the car.

***

Chapter 23

Rachel

I felt like an idiot, overwhelmed with emotions. I didn't want to cry because it wouldn't do anything to help me anyway. Every time my eyes threatened to release tears, I would replay that moment in my head, and I would stop.

***

I sat in the girl's bathroom as I felt the streams of tears make their way down my face. My face was completely wet at that point, and I was certain my makeup was messed up for the day. The twins were taking a test, so it was just me, left alone to suffer through my thoughts. I heard footsteps outside the stall, but I didn't mind them until they stopped right outside my door. I looked down at the feet, recognizing the designer boat shoes. They belonged to Taylor Morris. She had the audacity to knock on the door and disrupt my already disturbed peace.

"What is it, Taylor?" I grumbled.

"Rachel, why are you making a fool out of yourself in this bathroom?" she asked in her high pitched voice.

"You fucked the guy I was seeing, Taylor. What should I do? Shake my ass and celebrate?" I deadpanned.

"I mean, why are you crying?"

I opened the door and let it fall open to reveal my unamused expression. Was something not clicking for her? She regarded me with fake sympathy.

"Rachel, I know why you're upset. I get it. It's just that nothing will ever be able to beat the love Kadeem and I have for each other. It was a good try though. You put up a good six-month fight," she said.

"Taylor, just shut up," I snapped.

"But Rachel, I'm trying to help you. Those tears don't work for girls like you. I mean, look at you." She gestured rudely in my direction.

"What?"

"When people see me cry, they feel bad and help, but you're a strong black woman. You're supposed to power through. Ya know?"

"You're black too, Taylor," I said, pushing past her to the sink.

"Yeah, but look at me and then look at you," she scoffed.

It didn't take long for me to realize what she meant. She meant our skin tones, and I was mortified. With a smug shrug, she walked victoriously out of the bathroom.

***

It had been a few days since the morning in the woods. I had stayed mostly to myself. Nicole checked up on me a few times before she went back to the city, but I was pretty sure she had no idea how to actually help me. This was way past her *big sister expertise*, but I appreciated her attempts. Beyond anything else, she was a good person, and it was comforting knowing she was there. If it had been even a year ago, she probably would have been the only person I would want to be around if something as bad as this happened. It was different now. The main person I wanted around wanted nothing to do with me.

I'd worked out downstairs in the basement and was slowly walking upstairs to my room. The headphones blasted some upbeat pop music in my ears, and, for the first time in days, I was engulfed in something positive. When I saw Josh sitting at my door in a half undone button-down shirt and black pants, I was a little surprised to say the least. I turned off my music and tried to say something, but nothing came out. My hands started shaking in a mixture of anger and sadness. I forced myself to take a few deep breaths.

"Take a walk with me," he said.

We walked in strict silence. It wasn't because I couldn't speak, but I knew that if I did, I would never stop crying. And I was NOT going to cry for a man who probably thought what Taylor thought–that he was better because he was lighter. It was right before dusk and there was a calming light that luminated everything around us. Even so, I felt the opposite of calm.

When we made it to the clearing so we could see the river in the distance, I exhaled at the sight. The golden hour light over the water looked absolutely amazing. I wanted to take a picture, but I had forgotten my phone back at the house. It would soon be gone as I noticed the sun setting, along with heavy clouds rolling in.

"It's really beautiful, isn't it?" He sighed, but I didn't respond.

Josh was moving way too much to be enjoying the view, and I finally let myself focus on him. He grabbed some leaves and twigs, putting them into a pile of more twigs. I watched in confusion. He took out a lighter and started a fire in between us. It was controlled, but the city girl in me still felt uncomfortable. Fires were meant for stoves.

"What the hell are you doing?" I asked, breaking the silence, making him look up at me for a second.

"When I have some things on my mind that I have to let go, I do this," he said.

"You *burn* things?" I asked.

He shook his head. "It's more than that."

Throwing a couple more dry leaves into it, he nodded, satisfied, at the inferno between us. He wiped his hands on his pants before he slid them in his pockets. The sunlight began to disappear and the light of the fire seemed to glow brighter. I drew my attention upward and saw Josh staring back at me. The fire illuminated his face, and I wondered if anyone could argue that this man was not a work of art.

"Sometimes it's hard to let things go, but the idea of burning them and releasing them into the atmosphere makes me feel like I can finally move on," he explained, his voice soft.

I nodded, and he gave me a faint smile before continuing. He grabbed another leaf and held it between his fingers. His eyes watched the flames intently as he seemed to think about what to say next.

"I turned my back on my best friend when she needed me the most," he said before throwing it into the fire.

After a couple beats, I grabbed a leaf near my foot and held it up. Loud thunder sounded in the distance, but his gaze on me remained. I tried to speak, but instead, I just let out a sob. The tears started to flow out of my eyes, refusing to be stopped.

"Why?" I cried, "I didn't mean to. I didn't mean to, and I'm sorry."

I threw the leaf into the fire, and Josh walked around to me. He slowly rubbed my back, and it made me calm down enough to catch my breath again. He held another leaf up.

"I haven't been honest." His voice was barely more than a whisper.

I wanted to ask more, but I was too hysterical. I threw leaves in and just cried. Josh patiently watched by my side. I felt like an idiot as I threw in leaves and said nothing, but it was so calming to know he was there for me. It hadn't been the same without him.

"I'm sorry," I repeated, quietly this time.

"Don't be," he soothed in the same tone.

"I feel stupid crying," I breathed.

"Why?"

"My tears don't matter."

He took a step back to look me in the eyes properly. I stared back too as my lip still trembled. It didn't stop, as much as I tried to convince it to.

"Everything you do matters, Ray. What in the world made you think that?" he asked, upset.

"Life. No one cares about the tears of women that look like me," I said.

"That's not true. I do… I'm confused." His eyebrows furrowed.

"A lot of people don't when the woman is as dark as I am," I replied.

"What does your color have to do with it?"

"It has everything to do with it," I said, and Josh's expression looked so disappointed. For a moment, I regretted saying what I did. But then I realized it wasn't me who he was disappointed in.

"Rachel, the world is fucking stupid. There are absolute idiots that keep mindsets like that cycling through society. That's one reason why I was scared to come out of hiding. There are so many terrible realities like that out there. But, shit, I would do it all again if it means I get to do it with you… You're so beautiful and smart, and you make me laugh so much. I would endure the world's worst truths a thousand times just so I get to have you as my person," he finally said. More tears ran from my eyes. This time, it was for a different reason.

I wrapped my arms around him, and just like that, water began to pour out of the sky. The fire smoldered quickly, and we were drenched. It was dark now, but there was still enough light for me to make out his face. The fire was gone, and for some bizarre reason, it felt like this chapter, whatever it was—pain, suffering, confusion, was over too. Josh stared at me, and I watched as the water collected on his eyelashes before dripping down; how his now short hair got stuck on his head.

"I don't know what to say," I said, and I immediately wanted to throw myself off the nearby cliff for not being able to find better words than that; for not being able to kiss him like I wanted to. I never was one to hesitate in situations like these, but I just couldn't. It wouldn't have been right to kiss him right then and there.

"You don't need to say anything. Actually, you saying something *would be* appreciated, but it's okay if it's not now," he said with a wry smile.

I hugged him again. It felt safe and secure. Warm.

When we got inside, it was quiet. Our clothes were heavy with rain. Josh and I threw our heavy jackets on the floor next to the umbrella holder. The silence could have been awkward, but it wasn't. I knew Josh was painfully patient and would wait for a very long time for me to process, but I didn't want to take advantage of that.

"I should actually go shower now," I said, breaking the silence.

"Yeah same," he said, observing the very expensive looking shirt that was now pasted to his broad chest. I couldn't help, but look too. I didn't realize I was staring until I noticed him looking at me. I felt my cheeks warm up.

"By the way, how was the meeting today?" I asked, desperately needing to fill the silence.

"It was interesting. I don't know how Noah and Nicole do those all the time," he answered.

"Yeah, we definitely have to give them credit for that." I snorted.

He gave me a small smile that made me feel so many things at once. My heart was having a hard time regulating itself. I was about to excuse myself to finally go upstairs when my phone started to vibrate next to my keys on the table.

"Um, it says "Trash Can" is calling." Josh laughed.

"Hey, Rachel?" A familiar voice answered once I tapped the green symbol on the screen.

"Jason?" Josh asked with a laugh.

"What's so funny? Why is he laughing?" Jason asked.

"Nothing. What do you want?" I asked with the phone on speaker.

"Just checking up on you guys. I tried to call Josh, but he didn't answer his phone," Jason said.

"We're good, but why did you really call?" Josh asked with a raised eyebrow, and this time, I laughed.

"Really that! You guys are the worst. Anyways, I'm hanging up," Jason sighed.

"Love you too, brother," Josh said with a full teeth smile.

When he hung up, Josh's smile started to make me melt. Feeling overwhelmed, I decided to walk upstairs. When I got to my room, I locked my door and slid down to the floor. My head was submerged in emotions. *How did this happen? Josh had feelings for me?* I mean, of course he did because I was beyond fabulous, but it now made things complicated. Also, what would Nicole think? She already had so many reasons to be annoyed with me, but this could make her shun me from being her sister.

I was about to get off the floor to make my way to the shower, but my phone started to violently vibrate again. I looked at my phone, and Ashlyn's name shone brightly on my screen. It had been quite some time since we had spoken. My stomach twisted.

"Hello?" I answered.

"Bitch, where the hell have you been?" Ash's voice sounded.

"Ash, hey. I've been… upstate," I sighed, realizing it had been some months since I had gone to school in person.

"With Josh? Everyone on the team has been asking how you were since you said you would not be dancing this semester," she reported calmly, but I could hear the sadness there.

"Yeah, where Josh lives. I miss you," I said, meaning it.

"Can we come visit you in a few weeks? It's been forever."

"Is that Rachel? Tell her I'm going to punch her in the boob. Where the hell is she?" Ang's voice called in the background.

"I'm sorry, okay? It's been…" I trailed off. What words could even describe this whole ordeal?

"You don't have to explain. We're mainly joking. I'm really sorry about everything." Ash's voice was so soothing.

"Thanks. I wish I had words to explain, but I just don't have them," I exhaled, and it was probably the most honest thing I had said in a very long time.

"This is better than you not speaking. I remember you texting me that you couldn't get the words out. I was about to FBI your ass and figure out what your coordinates were," Ang snorted, clearly closer to the phone.

"I love you guys." I chuckled.

"We love you too! So… how's it been living with the hottest man we know?" Ash asked.

"Ash, he's practically family, but I kind of think I like him back, so I guess that's something. I don't know what to do," I continued, the words tumbling out.

"Shut up! Back? As in, he likes you too? I'm so jealous, I'm going to leave the country," Ang screamed.

"I'll buy the fucking tickets," Ash added.

"I don't know what I want to do," I sighed.

There was no response for a moment, and I held my phone up to make sure they were still there. They were, but they were silent.

"Okay, so Nicole is going to be upset. He's older, he's Noah's brother, and she's going to be super protective over you. She is not going to want you to rush into something while you're grieving," Ash said in a very matter-of-fact tone.

"But also Josh is gorgeous. *Like really just immaculate*. He's funny, he's sweet, and he cares about you.

He's also a great candidate to be the future Mr. Rachel Smith, ya know?" Ang countered.

I wondered if I could share my other reservations, the ones that I felt because of the Taylors of the world. Ash and Ang had always been there for me no matter what, and I wanted to trust them, so I did.

"There's also another thing," I said.

"What? He's too rich?" Ang asked, dryly.

"No. We're just so different." I chewed on my lip, laying my head back against the door.

"So? Opposites attract," Ash retorted.

"Yeah, but we're *different*. We grew up different. *We look different*. I'm scared he'll…" I began.

Ash interrupted, "He's not Kadeem, Rachel. What you're saying is completely valid, though. That was a really awful thing that happened. But also, I don't think Josh cares. Now, that's my idealist side coming out to speak for the maybe three interactions we've had, but I believe it to be true."

"Do *you* care what he looks like? I mean, you hang out with us, and people never know what the hell we are," Ang chimed in.

"No. Well, actually, yeah, I care if the guy I'm dating is attractive. And Josh is very attractive, but me being attracted to him has nothing to do with his skin being a certain shade," I said.

"Then, I say, go for it. I will add that I am severely jealous of you right now because the man is top tier, but I'm even happier for you," Ash soothed.

"There's nothing to be happy about. We're not together yet." I laughed.

"Well, yeah, but it's going to happen. I know you might need some more time after everything that happened, but don't deprive yourself from being happy," Ash said.

"Please get laid so you can be back on the team and dance in the fall. I don't know how you're surviving without dance, and I don't know how to entertain Ash anymore," Ang groaned.

It was funny, but it hadn't occurred to me that dancing might have been what I had been missing all along. I hadn't danced since December, and it was April already. I had been dancing for almost my whole life. In conjunction with everything else that had gone wrong, it made sense why my body would feel weird.

" I'm getting off the phone. Me getting laid has nothing to do with me being on the dance team." I chuckled uncomfortably.

"Oh come on, since when did you become a prude?" Ang laughed.

"It's different with him. He's my friend. This isn't just a random hookup anymore. If we get through this… I don't know. I feel like this would be endgame for us," I admitted, and the twins awed in unison.

"Okay Ash, I'm going to let you handle the rest of this convo. It's too sweet for me," Ang said, her voice disappearing from the other line.

"Girl, I have practice in the morning, but I will speak to you soon. I'm serious, we'll be coming to visit soon," Ash said before she hung up.

Chapter 24

Josh

I woke up the next morning to Jason and Eliza sitting in the living room. Eliza had her leg propped up on a pillow in a big cast as she sat on the couch. Jason sat in the recliner chair across from her. I must've walked in on some conversation that I wasn't supposed to hear because they both paused when they noticed me standing at the entrance to the room.

"Hi?" I said, but it sounded more like a question. Technically it was because I wanted to know what they were doing here.

"Hey, less annoying Westbrook," Eliza teased with a smirk. And it made sense, but also didn't since, I guess, that was never *really* my last name.

"Morning. How's your leg?" I asked as I stifled a yawn.

"I have another nine weeks to go, but I'm doing okay." She shrugged.

"Until then, she's crippled," Jason remarked.

Eliza rolled her eyes, and Jason chuckled. I rubbed my eyes and looked at my watch. It was only nine in the morning. Why was everyone so awake?

"When did you guys get here? And why are you here? No offense," I added.

"I needed a change of scenery," Jason said.

"I wanted to not fight with my mom," Eliza sighed.

"So we texted and decided to party with you and Rachel." Jason smiled.

I nodded and looked around. Rachel was nowhere in sight.

"She's not up yet?" I asked.

"I don't think so," Jason said.

I slid away and went to look for her. She wasn't in the kitchen or the office, so I went upstairs to go to her room. I knocked on the door, and, after a few seconds, she opened it. She gave me a small smile, stepping aside for me to come in.

"Hey," I said, attempting to sound calm.

"Hey, what's up?" Rachel asked.

"Nothing, what's up with you?" I asked, not sure if it was okay to sit.

"I just woke up a little bit ago. I heard we have company," she said dryly.

"I guess I'm not the only one who's not in the social mood," I felt a smile form on my face.

"No, you're not." She snorted, sitting back down on her bed.

I made my way over to her and sat on the foot of her bed. For a moment, it was silent, or at least as silent it could be with Jason and Eliza speaking loudly downstairs. Rachel hugged her legs to her chest, which made her appear so small. Her hair was in a bun on her head, and she was in a big t-shirt and shorts. She looked beautiful in anything.

"So, I've been thinking," she said, and I felt my stomach twist.

She looked down for a moment, and then her eyes met mine. She did nothing wrong, yet I felt like I was at gunpoint. She was about to pull the trigger, and after that, nothing was going to be the same. I took a deep breath, waiting for her to continue. Whatever she was going to say next, I knew my feelings for her wouldn't change.

"I took some time to think about what you said last night, and… Are you okay?" she asked, and it caught me off guard.

"W-what?" I stuttered.

"Are you good? You look stunned or like you're not breathing." She chuckled, the sound calming my nerves.

"I… don't know. I'll let you know when you're done," I sighed. She was either going to tell me that I was worthy or I wasn't.

"Okay, well, like I said, I've been thinking about it since last night. I had no idea you felt the way you did. I wish you told me before because I–" she began but was interrupted by heavy banging on her door.

I groaned and walked over to the door with every intention of punching whoever was on the other side unless they were notifying us of imminent danger. Behind the door was Jason, with a fist in the air, about to bang loudly on the door again.

"What?" Rachel asked from behind me in a voice so very different from the soft and soothing one she was using just moments before.

"Hey, we're going to go see the cherry blossoms and have a picnic down by the river. I'm going to drive us 'cause Eliza can't walk. Get dressed. We're leaving in twenty minutes," he asserted before he ran out.

My shoulders fell before I slowly turned to Rachel. She exhaled deeply before she stood up.

"Raincheck?" I asked.

"Yeah, raincheck."

The cherry blossoms were beautiful, except for the fact that they made me sneeze. Thankfully, I knew that and brought allergy medicine with me just in case. It didn't completely make the itch in my nose go away, but it made it bearable. Eliza set her crutches down against a tree and sat down on a large blanket we had set on the grass for her. Rachel rested next to her in a red dress, and they chatted amongst themselves. I remembered how much they hated each other when I had first met them, but it was clear that was no longer the case.

"How was the meeting the other day? I texted Nicole, and she mentioned that you did well," Jason asked me.

"It was okay. A couple of assholes, but they seem tolerable for the most part," I said.

"I'm not surprised about the assholes part. Since when do you curse?"

"Since when do you text Nicole?"

"I asked first."

"Since life got much more complicated and more colorful language seemed suitable," I answered.

"We've always texted. Believe it or not, we used to be super close, and we dated for a couple months. That didn't end up going well, but at least we're on better terms now," he said, and I could hear the pain in his voice.

"You know, you might find someone who actually mentally stimulates you as much as she does," I said, nudging him with my elbow.

"Yeah, but I don't think that's anyone I know right now," he sighed.

"It could be. You just have to be open to it."

"How are things with Rachel?" he asked, changing the subject.

"What do you mean?"

"We're still pretending nothing is going on there? Okay, got it," Jason deadpanned.

I gave him a pointed glare and warned, "No comment.", To my surprise, he respected it.

When we got back to the house, the sun was on its way down. Eliza made her way with her crutches over to the kitchen and grabbed a bottle of wine. She glimpsed over her shoulder and saw me watching her.

"Hello, aren't you going to help me get some glasses?" she asked.

"Are you supposed to be drinking when you're on pain meds?" I raised an eyebrow.

"What are you, the police? Anyway, no it's fine now that I'm off the heavy stuff," she said.

"Alright," I relented, grabbing four wine glasses and bringing them to the coffee table in the living room.

"Thanks," she huffed as she struggled to hold the bottle and get to the living room.

I put the glasses down on the table and ran back over to pick her up. She let out a yelp and dropped her crutches. She hugged the bottle as I placed her on the couch where I had found her this morning.

"Glad you didn't drop the wine." I chuckled.

"Come on, I have priorities." She laughed but then slowly stopped when she looked over my shoulder as I placed her leg on a pillow.

I turned around and saw Rachel standing in the entrance to the room. Her facial expression was unreadable. Jason walked out from behind her and entered the room.

"Ooh, we're drinking? This day keeps getting better," Jason grinned, rubbing his hands together.

"You're going to drink with us?" Rachel finally asked me.

"I'll have one," I said with a smile.

"Look at you. We've all been a bad influence," she said and shimmied her shoulders.

I rolled my eyes and sat down.

The night began with us snacking and drinking some wine. I very slowly nursed my first glass as everyone made their way to their second. I could tell the moment it hit everyone. Eliza became giggly and way looser than she usually was. Jason became even more animated. Rachel became touchy, and I found her pushing Jason's shoulder when he made a joke and leaning on me from time-to-time. I wasn't even sure when the second bottle came into play, but I eventually noticed it sitting like a centerpiece amongst us.

"We should play a game," Eliza said.

"What kind of game?" Jason asked, glancing up at her on the couch.

"Truth or dare!" Rachel called from laying down on my lap.

"Fantastic, I will go first because I say so," Jason announced.

"Wait, are you telling the truth or dare or taking one?" Rachel asked.

"Oh, I will give one. Eliza, truth or dare?" he asked.

"Truth. I do nothing for no one, but myself," she declared.

"I love that for you," Rachel chimed in.

"Hmm… Okay, why are you so fucking angry?" Jason asked.

Rachel began coughing and sputtered a little over her glass. She sat up straight then, and I patted her back. She threw a piece of popcorn at him.

"Don't be mean," Rachel warned in a very non-threatening, off-brand, baby voice.

"*I'm not.* I want to know. You literally hate everyone," he whined back.

"First of all, I don't hate everyone. Secondly, I don't have to smile because it makes you more comfortable. Life hasn't been kind to me, so why pretend that it has been?" Eliza answered.

"I hate that question. I vote Eliza gets a new one because you would never ask Noah a question like that. He doesn't smile much either. Joshy, get your brother," Rachel slurred a little.

I took Rachel's glass and handed her a water bottle instead. She gave me a little eye roll and took a few sips while staring straight at me. I winked at her. She smiled again.

"Okay, fine. How does it feel being a Craig? Do you like being an heiress? That's what a magazine called you once," Jason said, and I found it interesting that he knew that.

Eliza thought for a minute and then nodded a little like she had decided that it was a question worthy enough of her time.

"It's a lot of pressure. My mother wanted to be one way, and I'm pretty much the exact opposite. It started off as resistance to get her to let me do what I want, but it stuck, I guess. I don't like being an heiress. I'd much rather live normally. When you don't fit the little picture people have of what you should be like in their heads, it's disappointing for them," she said.

Jason looked like he was itching to ask more questions, but that's not how the game went, so he just nodded. Eliza put her hand on the top of his head and messed with his curls. He clenched his eyes closed as if he was bracing for her to pull each one out by the strand, but she didn't.

"Alright, it's my turn. Rachel, truth or dare?" Eliza asked.

"Hmmm, dare," Rachel announced confidently.

Eliza sat up again and gave a devious smirk. I was scared ,and it wasn't even my turn. But maybe it was because she was looking at me.

"I dare you to kiss Josh for thirty seconds," she proclaimed.

"WOAH," Jason hollered, making the room vibrate.

"Um," Rachel stammered, looking at Eliza in horror.

My jaw dropped as I gaped at Eliza. She threw her head back, her long red hair cascading along the arm of the couch. The laugh that left her body was loud. Jason appeared so restless that it looked like he was going to combust.

"You guys are so lame," I said.

I looked over at Rachel. She was downing the rest of the wine in her glass. I was frozen. I had kissed Nina a few times, but I'd never had an audience before. Being in this situation made me both elated and worried. I would've much preferred our first kiss to be at a time where I felt more confident. Rachel stood up on her knees to be at my face level and took my lips with hers. She put both of her hands on the sides of my face as her lips glided against mine. They were so soft and smooth. My eyes drifted close, and I realized how good she was at this. I wasn't sure why I didn't assume she would be. Becoming more at ease, I put my hand on her chin to tilt her head. She pulled me closer, and I complied. She had moved things over to just lip kissing to French kissing, and I was all for it. I had forgotten there were other people in the room until Jason shouted.

"That's time!"

Rachel pulled away first, and I reluctantly followed suit. We stared at each other for a second before we both looked away shyly. My head was reeling. I downed the rest of the wine in my glass. Eliza and Jason were wooing and making other excited noises. I glanced over at Rachel again and a ghost of a smile crept up on her lips for a second before she shook her head out of whatever thought she was having.

"You good guys?" Jason asked with a laugh.

I glared at him, and he smiled showing all his perfect teeth. I shook my head and just chuckled.

Chapter 25

Rachel

That night, I was restless. Josh and I barely spoke to each other after the kiss. I think we were both processing. And there was a lot to process. *A lot.* I didn't expect the kiss to be bad, but I definitely did not expect it to be like that. I laid down under my covers and thought about it that night. I scrolled on my phone as I tried to get my mind off it, but it didn't work.

I texted Nicole and Ash back to let them know I was okay. Omitting the kiss, of course. I needed time before I shared those details. I was just about to put my phone away when I saw a text from Josh pop up on my screen. My heart jumped.

Josh Crawford: You up?

Me: Yeah

Josh Crawford: Are you tired?

Me: No, I can't sleep. What about you?

Josh Crawford: Same.

I didn't know what else to say. Then I remembered that we had never finished speaking that morning. I think he had too because of the next message.

Josh Crawford: Can I come over?

It was not a big deal. Josh always spoke to me in my room. He even did the same when I was in my old house. It was never weird, but now it seemed different. A barrier had been broken. I wanted to appear cool about it, though. I needed to be an adult about the situation.

Me: Your house, your rules.

Josh Crawford: Your space, your boundaries, your comfort.

The man did have a point. For some reason, that made me like him even more. Judge me if you will, but I don't think a man had ever respected me as much as Joshua Crawford did.

Me: Okay, yes, you can come over.

A minute later, he knocked lightly on my door. My heart started to jump a little. I was sure that nothing was going to happen. Unless it did. But we weren't ready for that yet. I turned on my nightstand lamp before I tiptoed over to the door, letting him in. He closed the door quietly behind him.

"Hey," he said, in a smooth, low voice.

"Hi," I said.

We were silent again. I observed everything about his face. His long lashes, his small smile, the sharp edges of his jaw… I took everything in. It was slightly hard with the little light we had, but I made it work.

"You look cold," Josh pointed out, breaking my concentration. I was starting to shiver. The days were warm, but the nights were still chilly.

"Oh, I am a little. The temperature dropped," I admitted, wrapping my arms around myself.

"You should get back in bed." He chuckled, giving me a small once-over.

I nodded and got under the heavy comforter. My body was grateful for the instant sensation of warmth. He cautiously followed and sat on the foot of my bed. I noticed the goosebumps on his arms.

"You can get in here, too. I have space," I said before realizing that would mean he would be under the covers with me.

Josh's eyes searched mine. His expression, hesitant, unsure. Josh may have been older, but he was so much more innocent than me. I assumed that's why he looked so nervous, why his eyes took forever to meet mine.

"Are you okay with me being over there with you?" he asked as if I wasn't just about a couple feet away from him.

"Yes," I answered.

He nodded and got in next to me. The bed moved a little under his weight until he stopped moving. He was closer now but seemed to meticulously make sure that no parts of his body touched mine. For a few minutes, we sat in silence.

"It is really warm under here," he agreed.

All I did was give a small smile and nod. He was so close, and I was pretty sure I forgot how to breathe. I never got nervous around guys. Especially when it came to simply being in close proximity to them with nothing else going on. Why should I? They are humans just like us girls, but this was different. Josh was not a guy. Okay, he was definitely a guy. A gorgeous one, but he was just different. I felt a little out of my element, but I wasn't going to let it show. So, I did what I always did–made a joke.

"You can always take things off if you get too hot," I teased.

Josh's eyes slowly widened when he realized what I had implied. If it were bright enough, I'm sure I would've seen a blush.

"That's not why I'm here, Rachel." He chuckled.

"Then why are you here, Josh?" I asked, even though I knew he wasn't there for that.

"We didn't get to speak earlier, remember? I would love to get even a glimpse of what's going on in your head."

I nodded. It was now or never. I decided to just pull the band-aid off.

"I feel the same way. I'm scared, but I want you too," I said.

"Why are you scared? It's me. Are you scared of me?" he asked, seeming genuinely confused.

"Exactly, it's you…Your brother is married to my sister. They are going to feel weird if we date, don't you think?" I asked.

He shrugged. "Maybe, but I think there are worse things."

I nodded. It was quiet for a little while as we let everything sink in. If Nicole hadn't disowned me about everything else I had done, maybe this would not be the final straw for her. Unless, she decided that I had pissed her off for the very last time…

"Josh, how much do you like me? Like a little or a lot?"

"I love you, so I guess that could mean a lot," he said with a chuckle.

I gasped. How could he love me? I mean, duh, I was lovable, but *he* thought I was *lovable*. There was a difference.

"Oh, I didn't know," I said.

"How about you? How do you feel about me and this whole situation?" He searched my eyes and asked after a beat.

"I know I like you a lot," I confessed, wishing I had more to say, but I was still processing.

Josh nodded before planting a kiss on my forehead. It was such a simple gesture, but for me, there was so much meaning behind it. He appeared to be content with that answer, and that brought me some peace.

"Are you attracted to me? Do you like what you see when you look at me?" I asked, and I'm not sure why I did. He should if he loved me like he said, but I wanted to hear it anyway.

"Very.," he responded, "Are you attracted to me? You don't think I'm weird, right?"

"Well, I think you're weird, but in a funny way. Not in the creep way… So there's nothing about me that you would change or might make you change your mind a few months from now?"

Josh raised an eyebrow and froze where he was. I sighed. I knew he was going to pry it out of me. He wanted to know why I was asking these questions.

"Rachel, not that it matters, but you're beautiful. Why would I change my mind? Of course I wouldn't change my mind," he said, and his eyebrows furrowed like he had entertained something so ridiculous, but it wasn't.

"So you don't care that I'm darker than you?" I asked.

He snorted.

"Who cares?"

"Lots of people out there."

"The world is weird. I don't care about how dark you are. I didn't know you cared. Honestly, I didn't even know you would be considered dark. I haven't grown up around that way of thinking, and honestly, I just don't care… I care about you, not the color of your skin.

Actually, scratch that. I care because it's part of you, **and**, because it's yours, I love it, just like everything else about you. The way you talk, the way you walk, your smile, your hair, your eyes… I love it because it belongs to Rachel Smith," he admired softly, and all I wanted to do was kiss him as I let the words sink in and soothe something inside of me.

I nodded to show that I understood. We laid against my headboard in silence for what seemed like almost an hour. It was as if we were both processing everything that just happened between us. All I knew was that I wanted him to stay here. If not forever, at least for the rest of the night.

"So now what?" I asked.

"It's up to you," he said softly.

"What do you mean?"

"We could date, or we could be close friends for the rest of our lives. I want to be around you regardless," he said.

I leaned in and kissed him again, and he kissed me back. At first, we were so hesitant. Then, to my surprise, Josh broke the touch barrier first. He rested his hand on my thigh, and it was the first time something so small drove me crazy, in a good way. I knew it would eventually end at some point, but I wished to be in that moment forever.

The next morning, I woke up to the sound of rain steadily hitting the window. I checked my phone, and it was only six in the morning. Very little light shone through the thin curtains. I tried to grab my pillow from behind me to adjust it, but something kept me from being able to pull it. I grabbed it again, and this time, I heard a faint groan from behind me.

I turned around and saw Josh laying there fast asleep. For a moment, I had completely forgotten about us speaking and him coming over to my room. I watched as his chest rose and fell in the dim light. He was the definition of peace, and I knew there was no waking him up. I slid out of the covers and went to the bathroom. I brushed my teeth and threw on workout clothes.

I had snuck into the gym before. I did it whenever I wanted to not be bothered by others. Working out in solitude was my favorite. It's only you. Your energy. Your pace. Your vibes. I would workout alone when I had dance routines I needed to memorize. Sometimes the best company you could have when you need to hustle, is you.

When the workout was over, I looked at myself in the mirror. I was still me, but different. I didn't look different at all, but I felt like a different person, and for that reason, I felt as if I saw a different girl in the mirror. To finish my workout, I danced, danced, and danced.

I came upstairs from the basement, and it was still quiet. It was only a little after seven now, and dim morning light shone through the windows. It wasn't much, though, since the rain was still pouring down. I went to grab something cold to drink and saw Jason sitting down by the kitchen island. The smell of coffee was in the air. He picked up his cup to his lips as he scrolled on his phone. His hair looked damp like he had just gotten out of the shower. When I made it a few steps in, his eyes met mine.

"Morning," he said, amusement laced his voice. He always seemed amused about something.

"Hey," I responded as I made my way to the refrigerator.

"Sleep well?" he asked.

"Yeah, I slept alright. How about you?" I asked, grabbing a water bottle.

"Yeah, but I was up for a bit trying to listen to see what you and Josh were talking about *or doing*," he suggested, and I froze.

I threw my closed water bottle at him, but he ducked just in time. He started laughing triumphantly.

"You're so annoying!" I groaned.

"No judgment here! I knew something was bound to finally go down, especially after that kiss," he put his hands up to signal peace.

"Nothing happened," I argued, and unfortunately, it hadn't. After about twenty minutes or so of making out, Josh suggested we go to bed. At least one of us had discipline. I had none around him.

"That's a shame. There's been tension between the two of you for like a year," he said.

"What? No, there hasn't."

Jason didn't look at me, instead right behind me. I turned to see Josh standing there. He still appeared to be tired like he had just woken up.

"Morning, Rachel. Morning, *Jason*," he said with a touch of cold disgust, and it was more evident than ever that he and Noah were brothers.

"Morning," Jason sang in a tone that suggested so much.

"Oh stop, nothing happened. We were speaking. How did you find out anyway?" Josh asked through a yawn.

"I happened to be in the hallway coming upstairs when I saw you run into Rachel's room." Jason chuckled.

Josh looked over at me and shook his head in disappointment before he shook his head and went to the refrigerator to grab milk. Jason watched the both of us with a smile.

"I hope this becomes a thing. You guys are cute," Jason offered as he slid off his stool.

Josh didn't answer, and neither did I. I think we both felt like we had no privacy in the matter. When Jason was finally out of earshot, Josh turned to look at me. Before I could say anything, he pulled me in for a kiss. And I kissed him back.

"Josh, I'm sweaty. I–" I began to talk about how gross I was from working out.

"I don't care," Josh whispered, pushing me against the refrigerator, kissing me again.

I was lost in the kiss until I realized we could easily be found. Slowly pulling away, I evoked a noise of protest out of him. He finally opened his eyes and seemed to remember where he was too. I waited for him to say something, but his eyes were glued in the direction of the walkway. That's when I heard someone clear their throat. Standing in the walkway of the kitchen were Nicole and Noah. We really needed to stop doing things in the kitchen.

Noah looked slightly shocked while my sister looked absolutely horrified.

"What the hell?" Her voice loudly bounced off of every nearby surface.

"Nicole, hey, I was going to talk to you about this," I started.

"Talk to me about this? *This* is a *thing*?" Nicole asked.

"Yes, I mean no. I mean," Josh stumbled over his words, which made me super uncomfortable.

"It's not?" I turned as I asked him.

"Well, which one is it?" Noah asked.

"Did you know about this?" Nicole turned around and glared at him.

Noah's eyebrows almost met his hairline. The only thing I was convinced he was afraid of was my sister. He had seen a lot, but even so, nothing else would affect him in the manner that my sister did. I could tell from his pause that he had known something. I glanced back and forth between him and Josh, and they both looked very nervous.

"It was nothing near this the last time we spoke. I didn't know if it was going to become something," Noah said in a higher pitch than usual.

"Rachel, we didn't even define what this is yet. How would you like me to answer that question?" Josh asked, and I could tell he genuinely had no idea how to move in this situation. I would be his first girlfriend.

"How do you want to answer the question?" I asked.

Josh gave me a small, shy smile, and my heart started to melt. I found myself smiling and looking down. I wanted to jump and down excitedly, and also punch myself for how happy this boy made me feel. I even felt butterflies. That was a first.

"Rachel, in the office, right now," Nicole demanded.

I wanted to argue, but she already began walking there as if she expected me to follow. She was turning her big, bad, older sister voice on. I groaned and walked into the office behind her. I closed the french doors behind me and willed myself to look her in the eyes.

"What is going on?" She sighed.

"Josh and I kind of happened. I'm not sure when it started exactly, but it is definitely happening now," I said.

"You do realize that he's your brother-in-law's brother, and you're his sister-in-law's sister, right? That doesn't bother you?" Nicole asked.

"No, not really. Who cares? It's not illegal," I said.

Nicole sank into the large office chair and buried her face in her hands. I noticed a new ring on her ring finger. It caught every ray of light in the room. It was absolutely perfect.

"What's on your hand? You got a new ring?" I asked.

"Yeah, Noah asked me to marry him again. We're going to have a real wedding after graduation. He asked on my birthday," Nicole said, but seemed too sad to match her tone appropriately.

"That's amazing. Congratulations!" I smiled.

"Thanks, but no one is going to care now. They are going to be pissed about you and Josh," she said.

"I'm sure they will still care," I reassured her.

She shook her head in frustration . Her hair bounced around her shoulders as she moved her head in thought.

"I mean The Table," she sighed.

"So you're thinking about The Table instead of my happiness? Really, Nicole? Who gives a fuck about those old people who know nothing about the real world?" I exclaimed.

"If I keep them satisfied enough, I get peace. You wouldn't understand." She sat up, frowning

I watched as she patted the curls on her head. They were her own, but they looked like they were made perfect by some million dollar stylist. I watched as she dusted something off her white sweat set. She looked perfect all the time. Perfect hair, perfect outfit, perfect ring...

"You know what? You're right, I don't understand. I didn't get the perfect gene," I bit.

Nicole peered up at me with an expression that would have made sense if I had told her that the sky was green. She crossed her arms and gave me the most condescending head-tilt.

"I am not perfect," she said, humorously.

"You get everything. You look perfect. You're prettier, smarter, nicer... You're married. You're loaded. How can we even understand each other anymore? I'm sure you believe you would have dealt with the Tracey situation better," I exploded.

She made a facial expression that I was unable to read. I waited patiently for her to say something. I was waiting for her to mention what happened, but she just avoided it.

"I don't get everything. In fact, I miss out on a lot of things that I want. I don't have free time. I can't take full semesters so I've been taking classes every summer and winter intersession to make sure I can graduate on time. There are very few days when I just have time for myself. I have so many people to make happy… I'm rich, you're right. Noah has a lot of money, but the drawback is huge. I hate the word *perfect*. It's what Mom and Dad wanted me to be. Because of that, I felt like I could never take it easy because if I did, in my head, I would let them down. I had no idea how to deal with Tracey. I have no opinions on what happened because this was very much uncharted territory for me," she explained.

I didn't know what to say, so I listened.

"Rachel, I've always wanted to be fun and interesting like you were. You're beautiful. You're an amazing and talented woman," Nicole soothed.

"Woman? Wow, so if I am grown, why are you trying to get in between me and Josh?"

She rolled her eyes and let herself spin around a few times in the chair. A small smile creeped up on her lips. It wasn't because she thought it was funny, but because she knew I made a good point.

"Because he's older. He's your brother-in-law," she said.

"No, he's *your* brother-in-law. Not mine," I corrected.

"He's still older," she said.

"By a few years. It's not like I'm a baby, Coco. There is nothing that he's going to do that I don't already know about," I chuckled.

She grimaced.

"You're right. I have Derek to thank for that," she deadpanned.

"You knew what happened between me and Derek? I thought I covered that up well," I said, scratching the back of my head.

"I was depressed, not dead," she replied dryly.

"Give me and Josh a chance to figure this out, okay?" I asked.

Nicole just nodded, and I laughed because I saw so much of Dad in her at that moment. I knew him and Mom were probably there guiding us through all of this. I just hoped that they were somewhat proud of us. I smiled and turned to leave the office.

"Rachel, if he fucks up, I will have to kick his ass," Nicole called.

Chapter 26

Josh

I sat in the big, black SUV as it drove us to the CCT building. Some emergency meeting was being called into session, and Mr. Craig stated that I had to be there. Noah leaned his chin on his hand as we watched the buildings pass us by. He was especially quiet that morning. At first, I thought it was him in one of his moods, but I was starting to think his silence was directed at me.

"You ok?" I finally asked.

"Mhmm," he hummed in response.

"You sure? You seem upset," I said.

"Psh, well I'm always that," he snorted, "I just have a lot on my mind."

I nodded and looked out the window. I understood what that was like. Just a couple years ago, I really didn't have much to worry about. Nowadays, it felt like I worried as much as I breathed air.

"So Rachel is it? You sure?" He finally asked.

"Yeah, like how you are with Nicole."

"That's quite the statement to make. I might've felt that way because I had seen what else was out there," he said.

"I don't need to hop from girl to girl to know, like you and Jason," I fired back.

Noah narrowed his eyes at me, prepared to argue with my jab, but he nodded instead.

"Good choice… Make sure you speak to Nicole," he instructed.

Inside the meeting room, Mr. Craig sat with Greg and the two most annoying old men, Mr. Abbott and Mr. Elliott. They all stood up when Noah and I walked in. We sat down and began.

"Daniel, why am I being called in on a holiday weekend? It's Easter," Noah said in a professional tone.

"Since when are you religious?" Greg asked with a snort.

"I'm not, but I sure as hell shouldn't be here." Noah gave a smirk.

"Mr. Abbott reviewed some information in your father's will and trust, and we realized something was missed," Mr. Craig said.

Noah and I exchanged looks.

"And that was?" I asked.

"He states here that, 'my child or children will take on executive roles in The Table and its exercises'. That means that he wants both of you to take on duties, not just Noah," Mr. Elliott said before he handed Noah a sheet of paper.

Noah's eyes danced along the document. He sighed and then handed it to me. In this section, it stated that I was supposed to take on some of the responsibilities that Noah took on.

"So, now what?" I asked, bringing my attention back to Mr. Elliott.

"Noah is in charge, so your responsibilities will be discussed amongst you two," Greg announced with a small frown.

"Josh didn't ask for any of this," Noah said.

"Well, neither did you," Greg retorted.

Noah shrugged because that was true too. It was clear that he didn't ask for any of this, but made due with what he was given. Noah was a leader. I was not sure if I could do the same thing.

"And what if I say no?" I finally asked after a few moments of silence.

Mr. Elliott and Mr. Abbott rolled their eyes in sync, and it annoyed me just enough to hold my glare until they noticed me.

"And why on Earth would you do that?" Mr. Abbott finally asked.

"The board could vote for your funds to be frozen," Greg said.

"Can't I overrule something like that?" Noah asked.

"Not quite," Mr. Craig replied.

Noah and I exchanged looks again. His expression, full of sympathy. I just nodded and turned away. I knew his hands were tied. I just didn't know the rope was coming for mine too.

Chapter 27

Rachel

The house felt alive with the twins around. It had felt like so much, yet so little, time had passed since I had seen them at the same time. There was a time that we were connected to the hip, but it seemed almost unbelievable that so much time had passed since the fire. Had my mother and father really been gone for five months already? It didn't seem possible.

We sat in my room as we painted each other's nails and watched romantic comedies on the TV. I watched as the stereotypical kissing in the rain scene was being foreshadowed while I painted Ang's nails hot pink.

The hero and heroine started to confess their love for each other as the thunder roared, when we heard a knock on the door. Ash paused the movie with her hand of newly-painted red nails as I pushed myself off the floor. I opened the door and saw Josh standing there in one of his suits. His tie untied around his neck, his white shirt was buttoned down to the midpoint of his chest. I noticed how perfectly the navy blue of his jacket complimented his skin.

"Hey," he greeted me before furrowing his eyebrows at the sight of Ash and Ang.

"Hey, yourself. I thought you were coming back tomorrow," I inquired.

"I was supposed to wait for Greg to drive me, but I wanted to see you," he said softly.

"AWW!" Ang exclaimed in the background.

I gave Josh an apologetic smile, and he chuckled. He looked past me and waved.

"Hey Ash. Hey Ang," Josh said.

"Hey Josh," the twins both responded at the same time.

Josh tilted his head towards the hall, signaling that he wanted to speak alone.

"I'll be right back. Start the movie back up without me. I've seen this part before," I said.

Ang wagged her eyebrows at me before I closed the door. We went into Josh's room.

"What's up?" I asked.

"There's a problem, Ray," he exhaled deeply.

"Honestly, I'm more surprised when there is not a problem. What is it now?" I groaned.

"I have to be part of The Table, and honestly, I really don't want to," he grieved.

"Why don't you tell them? They can't force you to work. Can they?" I asked, but then I wondered if somehow they could.

"They will freeze my funds if I refuse," he said, frustrated.

"So that means you'd have nothing?" I asked. Somehow, I always forgot that Josh was loaded. He was just so normal. He barely ever wore anything super expensive like Noah and Eliza did. I liked him that way.

"That's more of a Greg question. I definitely have some money I get from investments and stuff, but I'm sure a lot would be gone," he answered.

I nodded and sat down on the foot of his bed. He studied me for a few beats before he sat next to me. I looped my arm around his and leaned on his shoulder. It was night by then, but he still smelled like his cologne—woodsy with touches of cinnamon. I could feel that his muscles were tense under his shirt.

"So what does this mean for us?" he asked.

"What do you mean?" I asked before I pulled away and looked at him.

"I mean, if I do this. If I start working for them, will that be the end of us?" He asked, and I could hear the vulnerability in his voice.

It was no secret that Noah and Nicole had to navigate situations that tested their morality and their relationship constantly. In the past, I had said that Noah had ruined all of our lives. I never imagined I would ever consider dating someone who had to do some of the same things he does. Part of me wanted to say that his circumstance would not affect our relationship or whatever was going on between us, but was that true? After everything, could I stomach this? Could I handle things the way my sister did?

"I need to think," I said, standing up.

Josh's head fell, before he rose it again with a blank expression. He nodded like he understood.

"Take your time," he said.

"It's not that I don't like you. It's just that–" I began.

"It's just that this might be too much," he answered. I didn't like that–when people put words in my mouth. How dare someone assume what I'm thinking? But I couldn't say anything because he was right.

I was about to speak when his phone started to ring. He looked at it and declined the call.

"I don't know," I sighed.

"Okay," he breathed, softly, like that was all he could get out.

His phone began ringing again. He breathed heavily as he glanced at the screen and tapped it before bringing it to his ear.

"Yes?" he asked.

I heard Jason's voice on the other end of the phone. The volume wasn't very high, so I couldn't make out his words.

"No, I'm not free right now," Josh said.

I could tell Jason's voice was in protest.

"Why don't we revisit this when I figure some stuff out?... Yeah, I'm fine... Yeah, I'm just not in the headspace," Josh admitted.

After a few more exchanges, Josh hung up and threw his phone to his pillow.

"Everything okay?" I asked.

"Yeah, it's just Jason up to one of his antics," Josh said, shrugging. "Anyway, I think I'm going to get some sleep. I have a long day tomorrow."

I nodded before I gave him a kiss on his cheek and left the room.

Chapter 28

Josh

I found Greg sitting in the living room the next morning. He was in a button down and gray slacks–he dressed like he always had to be within a dress code. His matching jacket was thrown over the back on the couch as he typed quickly on his laptop. That all immediately stopped as soon as he noticed me standing there looking at him.

"What's up?" Greg asked.

"Oh nothing, wishing Tracey took me out before this came up," I said and wished there wasn't so much truth to the words that just left my mouth.

Greg sighed. He closed his laptop and sat up, placing his feet on the floor. His eyes searched my face like all the answers were already there. Maybe they were.

"I wish this weren't happening," he admitted.

"You and I both," I said.

He exhaled deeply as he played with the wedding band on his finger. For a moment, I wondered what Greg's conversations with his new wife were like. Did he come home and tell her the crazy shit that happens, or did he spare her of the chaos? I hoped they had a sense of normalcy. I wanted that for Rachel and myself, but it didn't seem like that would happen. Well, maybe she could still have that, just not with me, I thought.

"I will say this, The Table is very different than it was a couple years ago. There used to be some unspeakable things that would happen, but Noah and Nicole, they really changed things the best way they could," Greg said.

"I believe that. They're good people in a bad situation. I just don't know if Rachel wants to be pulled into that. She's gone through so much because of The Table already. I can't even blame her," I admitted.

Greg nodded before rubbing his chin. He was thinking of something to say, but there wasn't anything *to* say. It was what it was.

"I don't think Noah would ever decide to put you in a position that would be uncomfortable. He knows this is not for everyone," he offered.

I noticed Greg freezing and looking over my shoulder. I turned around and saw Ashlyn standing in the hallway a few steps away from the foot of the stairs. She regarded both of us with hesitant eyes. I gave her a small smile. She smiled back and gave a small wave to Greg. He mirrored her one back at her.

"Hey Ashlyn, what's up?" I asked.

"Sorry to interrupt. I know it's early, but can I speak to you for a minute?" she asked, looking at me.

"Yeah, sure. Let's go for a walk. I'll meet you outside in a few," I said.

She nodded and went outside. I turned back to look at Greg. His eyes squinted in what seemed like confusion.

"I don't even know who is in this house anymore." He snorted.

"Rachel's friends, the twins, Ashlyn and Angelica, are here to visit," I explained.

"Well, enjoy your walk. I'm going to look through some applications," he said, patting my shoulder.

"Applications for what?" I asked.

"For two new assistants. You need one and Nicole needs a new one too," he replied.

I made a sour face and straightened my glasses.

"You're not going to help me anymore?" I asked.

"Always, but Noah is a handful and a half. I can only be in so many places at once," he said.

"How do you even find someone to do this job? 'Help wanted for an organized crime family'?" I scoffed.

"It's complicated. Surprisingly enough, Jason contacted me and applied for a position," he added.

I started to choke on the air I was breathing in. What the hell was he doing? He had been acting so strange lately, stranger than usual.

"You're *lying*," I exclaimed.

"Nope, he's actually interested," he said.

"I told him it was a conflict of interest, but he still wanted to schedule a time to discuss the matter further."

I groaned as I backed up out of the living room. Greg chuckled as his expression turned to one of irritation and picked up his laptop again. I went outside to see Ashlyn hugging her cardigan to her body. Her long, dark hair framed her face that was illuminated by the sun. She was pretty. I remembered when Rachel told me that Ashlyn had a crush on me. I didn't know how to react. She was a catch, just not for me. Looking back, it made sense why Rachel seemed almost relieved by my reaction.

"Hey, sorry about that. Is everything okay?" I asked.

Ashlyn stared at me in silence for a moment. I didn't know what that meant so I stared back uncomfortably.

"I wanted to speak about Rachel," she said.

"Oh, uh... okay," I hesitated.

"You like her, right?"

I wondered how honest I should be with her. It was way more than that, but would Rachel appreciate me saying that to someone else right now? Then again, they were best friends…

"I love her," I said softly, and it felt so good to say it that I felt myself smile a little.

"That's what I thought," she nodded.

"Well, I'm glad we have that settled." I chuckled after a few beats.

"Don't let her push you away. She's been super cynical when it comes to love lately because of everything that happened with Kadeem, but she does like you back. She's just scared," she said, and I could hear the concern and stress in her voice.

"I see. Did she say something that made you want to speak to me about this?" I asked.

"She just said that she's scared to trust that things will end up okay," she replied.

"Yeah, I get that," breathed, realizing that Ashlyn had no idea what that really meant. I too didn't know if things were going to end up okay. I don't think anyone wrapped up in this did.

"Yeah, well, I just wanted to tell you that. You're a great guy, and I don't want her to miss out because of everything that has happened. Between Kadeem being a complete asshole and her parents dying, she's had a rough past six months," she said.

I knew that, but I still appreciated knowing that Rachel had good friends in her corner. It's like how I had Nina, Nicole had Michelle, and Noah had Alex. Friends like that were essential.

"For sure. I appreciate you coming to me, Ashlyn," I said.

"Ash," a voice called from behind me.

I turned to see Angelica, Ashlyn's twin sister. She was in sweats and had her hair up in a bun. She gave me a closed mouth smile.

"Hey, we were just speaking about Rachel," Ashlyn said.

"I hope you guys date and bang a lot. She deserves it," Angelica shouted, and I felt my eyes widen.

"I don't know what to say to that." I laughed.

"Also, make sure you tell her that she's beautiful. She got fucked up by Kadeem because he was really color struck. His on-and-off girlfriend, Taylor, pretty much told her that she didn't get him because she's dark. The whole thing sucks, but she hasn't been able to shake it," Angelica added.

"I didn't know," I admitted.

I knew colorism was a thing. I read about it online and knew it caused a lot of division among people of color. It was just never something I'd had to deal with firsthand. It didn't matter what shade Rachel was, but I didn't realize that maybe it did to others. I looked at the twins as I thought about all the pain their friend had felt lately. Then it connected, this was why Rachel asked me if I cared what she looked like. At first, I thought it was a strange question because she knew I had a hard time even understanding the hate that some people held, let alone something so superficial as difference in skin shade. Now it made sense.

"Anyway, we're going to go back inside. She probably wouldn't want us telling you all her past traumas, but we want this to work," Ashlyn said.

"Anything to get our best friend laid by a hot guy." Angelica winked.

Ashlyn hid her face in her hands, and Angelica began to laugh. I shook my head. I thanked them and went inside.

I took some time to call Nina back. I was bracing myself for the lecture she was going to give me when she answered. When she did, she answered the phone in her soft, calm voice.

"Hey you," she greeted.

"Hey, I've been meaning to call you back. It's been a while," I said.

There was a pause on the other end of the call, and I waited uncomfortably for her to tell me I was an awful friend.

"That's okay… I have a confession," she sounded uneasy.

"Uh, okay," I said, not expecting her to say that.

"You promise that you won't get mad?" I hated that question because how would I know? I might after you tell me.

"Sure," I deadpanned.

"So, you remember the last time I was there? In the fall?" She asked.

"Yes, I do," I said, feeling something weird in my stomach.

"So, Jason was there and you were really wrapped up in whatever was going on with Rachel. And I was sad that you, kind of, shut me out, and so I hooked up with Jason," she blurted.

I let myself fall back on my bed. I was not mad. I was not jealous. I was not anything. I honestly did not know how to compute something so repulsive. I was also confused because hook up always had two meanings. In my head, it either meant what Rachel and I had done, and what we had not done yet. I hoped that it was not the latter.

"What do you mean by hook up?" I asked, though I wasn't entirely sure I wanted to know the answer to that.

"We… had sex," she said, and I wanted to throw up.

"Nina Perez… why the hell?" I asked loudly.

"I don't have any good reasons, but it happened, and I'm sorry," she squeaked.

"I have to go," I sighed.

"Josh, wait–" she began.

"Sorry, I have to go."

Chapter 29

Rachel

By the end of the week, I was in the house all alone again. Well, I wasn't completely alone. Caesar was around making sure I was alright every few hours. When the evening hit, I found myself sitting in the kitchen as he fixed a stir fry for me to eat for dinner.

"Caesar, how old are you?" I asked as I looked at the peppered hair on his head.

"I'm sixty-two," he responded.

I nodded. He looked over his shoulder like he wanted to ask me the same question, but decided not to.

"I'll be nineteen in a couple months, if that's what you wanted to ask," I offered.

"No, not that, Ms. Rachel. I… Nevermind," he said.

I frowned, now curious to know what the question was.

"Tell me," I protested.

"I really shouldn't pry," he hesitated as he gave me an apologetic frown.

"It's not prying if I want you to ask."

His shoulders relaxed at that.

"You and Mr. Josh have gotten close," he said.

"We have," I agreed, encouraging him to go on.

"So you two are an item now?"

"I'm not sure." I shrugged.

He nodded like my lack of further details made complete sense to him. I looked down at my laptop screen and continued typing my essay. It was due in a few hours, and I was not where I needed to be.

"He's always thought that he would be alone. I'm glad he has you. You make him so happy. I see it, and it makes me happy too. He's like a son to me. He's so good and pure-hearted," he said suddenly.

I smiled and stared at him for a moment. I could see in his glossy eyes how much love he had for him and how genuine he was being. It almost made me cry, but for more reasons than one. It made my heart swell that I was able to be the one to make someone like Josh happy, but I was also happy that he was cared for by someone who cared so deeply for him. As alone as he felt sometimes, at least he had that–balance.

"Thank you, Caesar." I smiled.

The next afternoon, I heard the doorbell ring. I saw Nina standing out front and opened the door. She looked beautiful in a low-cut green tank and loose jeans. Her long fingers pulled a couple strands of hair from her eyes. Other than that, her hair looked immaculate. It was shiny and looked like it had just been trimmed. Her cheekbones were framed perfectly.

I gave her a small smile, but it was not returned. She looked ever-so-slightly disappointed to see me there. It reminded me of the last time I had come to the house and had seen her.

"Hey, Nina," I gave her my best smile.

"Rachel," she said in a way that almost sounded like a sigh.

"Are you here for Josh?" I asked, even though the answer was obvious. She most certainly was not there for me.

"Yeah, I am," she said.

"Sorry, he's not here. Would you like to come in? We could call him and see—" I began, but she put her hand up to stop me.

"That won't be necessary. I was just driving by, but I should get going anyways. Um, thanks though," she said, taking a step back.

I did not know what to say. I never felt like Nina hated me, but I knew she didn't like me either. There was no doubt I cared about Josh. If I needed to make sure everything was alright between myself and Nina to make sure he was happy, then I would do it. I wasn't trying to be best friends with her, but we could at least be cordial. At least I had the mental space to even think about things like this.

"Nina," I called, walking out the front door and closing the door behind me as I followed her, "are we good?"

Her lips parted, and her head tilted in confusion.

"Good? Yeah, we're fine. Why wouldn't we be?" she asked.

"Because it doesn't seem that way. I don't know, you just always seem slightly pissed when I'm around," I said.

Nina just stared at me for a moment and said nothing. It seemed like she was caught off guard and had no interest in giving me any clarity. Not that she owed me anything, but it would've been appreciated.

"Um, yeah, I don't know what you're talking about, but I should go," she stammered.

"Okay," I said. What else was there to say?

I stood on the porch as I watched her throw her bag into her little black car and get in. When she started to back out, I went back inside the house. It wasn't thirty seconds before I heard the bell ring again. Nina was on the other side of the door and she gave me a defeated look.

"Actually, can I come in? It'll only take a minute," she said.

"Yeah, sure," I nodded, stepping to the side for her to walk in.

"So, you're right. I know that sometimes I must act weird because I do feel weird around you. It's nothing you did, not really. Things are just different between Josh and I, and I know you have something to do with it," she said.

"I think it's great you two are friends. I would never get in between that," I said earnestly.

"But the thing is, you did. Not on purpose. Josh put you there, and I am taking forever to get past something that is inevitably going to happen. Plus, I haven't been the best friend either," she admitted.

I shook my head. I was completely lost and nothing was connecting. What did she mean by the inevitable or that Josh put me there?

"I still don't understand."

Nina sighed before she continued.

"So… I can't believe I'm saying this, but you do know that at one point Josh thought he and I would date, right?"

"Yeah, he briefly mentioned it and then said you two realized that you were better as friends."

"Well, I always hoped that maybe he would change his mind, and at one point, I figured that he would. Then, you came along and slowly, I began to realize that I did not stand a chance."

"Me?"

"Yeah, you. He is so, so in love with you. I saw it before he did, and I had to watch him slip away from me—the only man I ever truly loved. Anyway, I think he's been making you more of a priority, and he's made it clear that you will always be put first. And if you two are going to be a thing, that's fine. I mean, I guess we're growing up now and boundaries have to be established, right? I think I just get jealous sometimes. I do stupid stuff when I'm jealous," Nina said.

I was frozen in place. That's it. No words, and certainly no movement.

"You do know he loves you right?" Nina asked.

"Yeah, kind of, but it's different when someone says they see it too," I said softly.

"I get it. Look, Rachel, I'm sorry for how I behaved. It was not right. You're really cool, and I'm glad Josh has finally found his person. Also, I'm really sorry about your parents. Josh told me that's why he had been

M.I.A., and I knew I should've been understanding, but I wasn't."

"Thanks," I gave her a grateful nod.

"You're welcome. Oh, and Rachel? Don't break my best friend's heart. You have all the power to break him, but even more to build him," she said, and with that, she was gone.

After a night of finishing assignments, I went down to the gym to blow off some steam. I had my earbuds in and was listening to some music to get me in the zone. When I opened the door to the gym, I saw Josh there. I stumbled back a little. It had been days since I had seen him, and I didn't hear him come back into the house. It wasn't like things weren't weird between us. I had left him hanging. Still, he gave me a shy smile before he went back to doing pull-ups.

I went over to the treadmill and started to jog. It didn't feel completely silent since I had music blasting in my ears, but it was unlike us to not be cracking jokes at each other. I turned the speed and resistance up on the treadmill and began to run. All I wanted to think about was running until the little dot on the screen reached the other side of the line it was on. When I finally got there, I lifted myself up and put my feet on the sides to turn it off. I looked to my side, where Josh was sitting, doing bicep curls with a weight I would have never imagined picking up. It was arguable that one weighed as much as Nicole and me combined. His arms flexed as he brought it closer to himself and relaxed as he extended his arm. I realized I was staring when I saw him looking up at me. I saw his lips say something as I watched him glow from the sheen of sweat on him.

"What?" I asked as I turned down my music.

"I asked if I was distracting you," he replied breathlessly.

"No," I lied blatantly to his face.

He nodded before switching arms. I moved over to the mats and began doing crunches. After a few reps, I reached for my bottle of water. My abs burned, but in a good way. I looked up to put my bottle back on one of the benches when I saw Josh watching me. He had a towel over his neck now and looked dry and back to normal. I turned my music down again.

"It seems like now I'm the one distracting you." I chuckled.

"You said I wasn't distracting you." He pretended to gasp.

"I never said you did!" I laughed.

"Fine, fine, okay… I'll be the honest one here. Yes, I am distracted," he teased, and I laughed more.

"At least one of us is honest," I deadpanned.

"Mhm, I'll take one for the team. It's hard to concentrate when Rachel Smith is just over there doing her thing," he casually flashed an eyebrow and I felt my heart jump.

"And why is that?" I asked as I walked over to the dumbells near him to pick up some tens and not the fifty-fives he was using.

"Because you're… sexy and nice to look at," he confessed, unsure. I wondered if he had ever said that to anyone else before.

"Thanks," I said, trying to hide the goofy smile I felt fighting to break free.

I glanced back over at the rack, and my brain must have turned into mush because I had completely forgotten what I had gone there for. Did I want dumbbells? If so, what weights? Before I knew it, Josh was behind me and his arm grazed mine as he picked up two ten-pound dumbells. When I turned around to face him, he handed them to me.

"Uh, thanks. How did you know I wanted these? What if I wanted your fifty-fives?" I asked.

"You never put the weights back. Whenever I see the tens on the floor, I know you were around not too long ago. But hey, if you want mine, feel free to go at it." He chuckled.

I dropped myself down on the bench across from him and rolled my eyes. He just smiled and looked away, but all I wanted was for him to look at me again. Although, his gaze felt like light burns on my skin. I came to the conclusion that I was completely losing it.

"Anyway, smartass, how was the city?" I asked, changing the subject as I started to lift a dumbbell with my right hand.

Josh looked up for a moment as if the ceiling were going to give him the answers. I found myself staring at him as he thought. He had facial hair growing in again, and I decided I liked him with some hair on his face.

"It was alright. Noah and I are still trying to figure things out," he said.

"I see. Things like what?" I asked, trying not to show the concern in my face.

"Like my role and what he has done to make their practices more ethical," he said, letting his eyes fall back on me.

I realized that I wasn't doing much with the weights, and I put them down next to my feet. I saw Josh's mouth quirk up in a smile, so I stood up to put them back on the rack. I walked back to grab my water bottle and stood awkwardly. Josh stood up too and now towered over me.

"How have you been?" he asked, breaking the silence.

"I've been okay. I need this semester to end," I sighed.

"You have about two more weeks, right?"

"Yes, and then ten weeks of freedom," I said.

"We'll celebrate, then," he offered softly.

I could have imagined this, but it seemed like he took a step closer. His eyes stared into mine, and it felt as if he could see into my soul. He leaned in, and I leaned in. I closed my eyes as I waited for his lips to touch mine, but they didn't. I almost whimpered from the deprivation.

"I should hop in the shower," he said in a whisper.

I felt my shoulders fall. Why didn't he want to kiss me?

"Yeah," I cleared my throat, "me too."

He started walking toward the door but paused right before he got to the threshold. I prayed that maybe he had changed his mind and simultaneously beat myself up for being this whipped over a guy.

"Good night, Ray," he breathed, and my chest immediately began to hurt.

"Good night, Josh," I managed to get out, and he was gone.

My frustration grew as the night went on. I stomped to the shower and aggressively soaped and rinsed myself under the shower head. Then I dragged my t-shirt over my head and threw myself onto my bed. I picked up my phone, but I didn't feel like bringing anyone else into this.

I stood up and walked over to Josh's room. I knocked on the door and said it was me. A few seconds later, Josh opened the door with a white towel tied around his waist. I took a moment to admire everything that wasn't covered but stopped when I noticed him looking at me expectantly.

"Can we talk?" I asked.

"Yeah, sure. Come in," he said, stepping aside.

I walked in and stood in the middle of the room. It was beyond big, and in this particular moment, I felt even smaller.

"What's up?" Josh asked casually as if he didn't know he looked the way he did. Maybe he was more oblivious than I thought.

"Are we okay?" I asked.

"What do you mean?"

"You didn't kiss me earlier. Why not?"

Josh chuckled and crossed his arms over his chest as if the question was obscure, but it wasn't.

"Did you want me to?" he asked, and I snorted at the question.

"Yeah, of course I do," I said.

Josh stared at me for a moment and gave me a once over. I wanted to fidget with my shirt but decided against it. Instead, I crossed my arms over my chest and waited for him to say something. After a minute, he dropped his arms and slowly walked over to me.

He grabbed my face and kissed me. It was the type of kiss that made your legs go weak, and the only way to stay upright was to hold on to him. When he pulled away, I took a few steps back before I found balance again. He stared at me for another second before he went into his bathroom and closed the door behind him. I couldn't find the power to move, so I stood there looking at the door until he came out. When he emerged, he had on pajama pants, but no shirt. I was grateful.

"The reason why I didn't kiss you wasn't because I didn't want to," he admitted.

"Okay, then why didn't you?" I asked.

"Because you said you needed time to think about what you wanted. Why would I kiss you when that could falsely influence that?" He shrugged, and I wondered if he was aware of what his muscles did when he did that.

"I know, but I don't want you to stop," I almost whined and I hated myself for it.

"Well, are you telling me you want things to continue?"

"I don't know," I said.

"Why not?"

"Because… The Table."

"And what else? None of us here are innocent anymore."

"And… What if you change your mind?" I finally asked softly.

Josh's lips parted like he wanted to say something, but then he closed them. His eyes looked sad for a moment before he walked closer to me. I felt my heart race. He stopped just a step or two away from me.

"Ray, that could never happen," he exhaled deeply like the very thought of it pained him.

"How do you know that? How am I supposed to know that? Why should I believe this is just not some temporary feeling both of us have?" I asked.

He shook his head.

"Because… You know, I always had this feeling that in some capacity you were going to mean something of substance to me. I was glad I was right, and trust me *I really* wanted to be right. No one has ever made me feel like how you make me feel. I don't just have feelings for you, I burn for you. And everyday, I burn more. I would confusedly hear stuff like this from Noah, and all I wanted to do was feel those things too, until I did. And it was worth the wait. Ray, I would do anything to make sure you have the world, if that's what you want. Anything *except* just be a means to an end. I think if I get any deeper and realize that's all I've been to you–a way to get through the crazy past four months or a way for you to move to someone else–I will not come out of this the same man. So, tell me where I stand."

For a moment, I was just stunned. My silence and fear were hurting him. It was written all over his face. I could hear it in his voice. Something that was once so sure and sturdy, sounded so shaken. After everything, was I ready for this? Something told me that we would be here for the long haul, and there was something so peaceful yet terrifying about that at the same time.

"I'm scared," I whispered.

"Sometimes it's the scary decisions that are worth making," he said.

For a moment, my mind drifted off to a memory from a year ago.

***

"Knock, knock," Dad said by my ajar bedroom door instead of knocking. He would always do that to me to make me laugh. I gave him a small smile, and he came in. He sat on the side of my bed and gave me a frown. It was prom night, and Taylor, Kadeem's ex-girlfriend or maybe current girlfriend at that point, ruined my plans for the night. Everyone was so sure we would be going together, and that ended up not being the case.

"I'm sorry about what happened," he said softly, breaking the silence.

"Thanks Dad. I wish I had more to say," I replied.

"That's okay. I understand. I'm still going to request you put your dress on, though," he said.

I sat up and gave him the most incredulous look.

"Is this some form of self torture?" I asked.

"No, it's not." He chuckled.

Then, Nicole came through the door with a large makeup bag in one hand and a curling iron in the other. My jaw fell a little in disbelief. I didn't even know she was home. She gave me a casual smile before she walked over to my vanity and started emptying the contents of the bag out on its surface.

"Excuse me?" I questioned.

"We're going to prom, girl," Nicole said.

"When did you even get here?" I asked.

"No time to worry about the logistics. We have forty-five minutes," she announced.

"I *don't want* to go to prom," I argued, rolling my eyes at how ridiculous everyone was being.

"We're not going to school. Just trust me," she said.

I looked at Dad, who had a happy expression on his face. He knew what was happening too. I could see him pushing me to face everyone at school, but Nicole definitely wouldn't. She knew what it was like. She just graduated the year before. I slowly sat down in the seat and let her do my hair and makeup.

In less than an hour, my hair was styled perfectly, my face looked perfect, and I was in my dress. I rolled my eyes, and Nicole broke her usual demeanor and jumped up and down happily.

"You look so beautiful," she gushed.

"Thanks." I smiled.

"Alright, let's show Mom and Dad in the yard," she said, pulling me along.

"Slow down, Coco. I can only walk so fast in this!" I chuckled.

When we got down the stairs, I heard a familiar voice in the air. It was faint and clearly was coming from outside. When we got through the patio doors, I saw Josh speaking to Noah. They stopped when they saw me. Noah gave me a little whistle of approval.

"You look amazing," Josh said.

"Thanks," I said, surveying the yard, noticing that it was decorated with my school colors.

"What do you think?" Josh asked.

"This is so nice. Who did all of this?" I asked, looking around.

"Mainly Josh. We all heard about what happened with prom, so he came up with the plan to do this in the backyard," Noah said.

"I called Ashlyn and Angelica. They promised that they would come by later," Josh added.

I simpered before I threw my arms around him and gave him a big hug. That's when I noticed his suit. It was all black and his pocket handkerchief matched the coral colors of my dress exactly.

"Josh, this is so nice," I told him.

I saw Noah turn away from us with wide eyes. I turned to see him gawking at my sister. She had on her prom dress from the year before. Normally, I would have been upset that the attention wasn't all on me, but I was happy that he got to see her in it. If Noah could, he would have jumped at the chance of taking her to prom. Nicole beamed as Noah kissed her on the forehead.

"Okay, I need pictures! Josh and Rachel, you first. You two look so cute," Mom exclaimed as she placed me in front of him. Josh chuckled, and I couldn't help but do the same.

Josh asked me to dance. When we got out in the middle of the yard as the music played, he put a hand in the center of my back and I put my hand in his. At first, it was clear he had no idea how to dance, but soon his steps kept in pace with mine.

"Having fun?" he asked.

"I am. Are you?" I asked.

"Yeah, but my focus was on you having a good time. I don't think I could let this day go by without doing something for you," he admitted, and it made me simper again. I knew I was so lucky to have someone like him as a friend.

"Plus, now you get to experience prom, kinda," I said.

He smiled, and I got closer to lean on him. He seemed to tense at first, but he eased before I thought to pull away. He wrapped his arm a little tighter around me, and I felt so at peace. It was such a foreign feeling, and all I knew was that I didn't want to know what it would be like to not have him around anymore.

***

Was that how it felt like when you found your person? I began to smile, realizing Josh was in the same predicament. He had no idea what to do here. He had never been in love before, but he was trying anyway. He deserved so much credit for that. Here I was, with way more experience than he had, and I was stuck. I began to laugh.

"What?" Josh asked uneasily.

"All this time, I was stuck and wasn't sure what to do. Part of it was fear of what could happen, but also a lot of it was that I also have no idea what I'm doing here. I don't think I've ever felt this way about someone before," I said, and Josh's eyebrow went up.

"And what feeling is that?" he whispered.

"In love," I said.

Chapter 30

Josh

Nicole was back at Soteria, which meant I finally had to speak to her about me and Rachel. Noah wanted me to do it, and it *was* the respectful thing to do. Nicole and I were close in some ways that Rachel and I weren't. I felt like I owed her a conversation at least.

When I got into the office that morning, Nicole was sitting in a short sleeve, fuchsia dress. She looked amazing as always, but there was something extra special about how she looked today. I stopped for a moment, wondering if she was on a video call or something. When I did, she heard my footsteps and waved for me to come in.

"Morning." She smiled.

"Morning, what are you all dressed up for?" I asked.

"Noah and I are taking our "save the date" photos in about twenty minutes."

"Aren't you two already married?" I raised an eyebrow.

"We are, but we're going to have a proper wedding after we graduate. It's early, but we're doing things in steps since our schedules suck right now," she sighed, but still smiled. It perfectly sums up our world. It can be unquestionably horrendous, but there are always reasons to smile.

"That's great! Well, congratulations then," I said.

"Thanks, but what's up? It's kind of early. The only reason I'm up is because we have to take these photos by the river before Noah's meeting at nine," she continued.

"I wanted to speak to you about something important, if that's okay."

Nicole nodded and gestured for me to sit on the couch across from her desk. She rested her chin on her palm and waited for me to speak with an uneasy expression on her face. It seemed like she almost knew what I was going to say.

"So, I want your blessing," I said.

"For?" She asked.

"Rachel and I are seeing each other now, and I wanted to speak to you about it," I said.

Nicole dropped her shoulders and looked at me warily. I found myself biting my bottom lip as I thought about all of the possibilities of what she might say next. Nicole was the nicest, but I knew she had a fiery side like Rachel. There had to be a reason why Noah was afraid of her at times.

"Josh, you know I love you, right? You are such an amazing guy, and I don't think I could ask for someone better to be my brother-in-law," she said.

"And I love our friendship too. Who else am I going to speak to about books and have them actually care?" I chuckled.

She smiled slightly and said, "But Rachel is my sister, and she's the only person from my side of the family who is left. I can't have anything happening to her. That includes older men breaking her heart."

"I completely understand, and I have no intention of breaking her heart," I went on.

Nicole didn't look quite convinced. She played with a Newton's cradle on the desk. Just like the ongoing momentum of the device, she was going to be unyielding in her hesitation until I opened up about how I really felt. I was aware that she and Rachel had already spoken about it, but it felt wrong never bringing it up. Nicole was my friend.

"When I met your sister, I didn't know what I felt. All I knew was that somehow, she would always be important to me. And I was right. To be very clear, Nicole, I wasn't looking to fall in love with her, and we didn't initially. She was the girl that I loved to annoy, and we became friends. Very quickly, I realized our friendship was incomparable, but then even sooner, I realized there was more. I'd never been in love, and at first, I had no idea what was going on. I thought, shit, this is weird. All I want is to make sure she's happy, and I'm completely enthralled in everything she does. Why is she the only one who feeds my fire? Why is she the only one my fire burns for? Why am I willing to put my fire out just so she can be okay? Then I realized, it's the type of things you and I read about in those old books. I understood it before, but I completely *grasp it* now. It's why it didn't work before. It's because I needed to meet Rachel. She made it all make sense. Anyway, I just wanted to ask for your blessing because we both care about you so much, and I don't think either of us can imagine life without you being there as much as you are present now," I confessed, and I could feel tears fighting to break free from my eyes. I kept them in though.

Nicole, on the other hand, looked like she was about to cry. At first, I wasn't sure how to react. Was she upset? Maybe she was mad. She stood up and sat down next to me. Before I could realize what was going on, she was hugging me.

"You love her?" Nicole asked breathlessly.

"Yes, more than my words could ever do justice to, but I will make sure that she knows everyday that I do," I said, hugging her back.

"Then who am I to stand in between that? You have my blessing, but honestly, Rachel would have gone on without it." She laughed.

"Well duh, but I would've been sad about it," Rachel's voice sounded.

I turned around and saw her standing by the doorway. Nicole let me go, and I walked up to her. Her eyes were wet like she had been crying too.

"What's wrong?" I asked.

Before I could say anything else, she got on her toes and pulled me in for a kiss. I kissed her back and tilted her head upward, but soon heard Nicole clear her throat. We both looked over at Nicole who was fanning her eyes with her hands.

"If you guys make me mess up my makeup, I'm going to be pissed!" She chuckled.

"Are you excited for your pictures? Where's Noah? I thought we would be outside already," Rachel said.

"I am. I just want a few sunrise shots. And that's a good question. He should be here by now," Nicole strained her neck to look down the hallway.

"I'm here, sorry," Noah called, walking in.

"Where were you?" Nicole asked.

"I just spoke to Greg, and he's a fucking genius," he said, excitedly.

"I don't disagree, but why?" she asked as she dusted off his suit jacket and low-buttoned shirt.

"I'll tell you later. Let's take some pictures, baby," he said before kissing her.

Later that day, Noah updated me on his conversation with Greg. Greg did a deep dive in my dad's documents and found that I could have a large role in either The Table or CCT with minor dealing with The Table. I chose the latter, of course. I was very into technology, but not so much into organized crime. Noah chuckled when I explained that to him.

"I get it, so with that being considered, would you like to be CCT's new CTO?" Noah asked.

I raised an eyebrow in confusion. There were too many acronyms for me to keep up with.

"What's that? I'm trying to think about words that involve illegal happenings to fit the acronym, but I got nothing," I said.

"Chief technology officer—" he rolled his eyes "—You would be in charge of our technology department. Anything that involves the technology our company uses will have to go through you."

It didn't take much for me to agree. The salary was just an extra bonus. Plus, I had minimal involvement with The Table. Noah was stuck in that, and to be a good brother, I did tell him to say something if anything crazy came up.

We were going over my technicalities when my mother called. I excused myself and answered her call outside.

"Hey Mom," I said.

"Joshua, how are you? How's Jason?" she asked.

It was summertime, and that meant everyone had more time. Jason finished school in two years and was celebrating before starting law school. Eliza was interning in the theater district and spent weekends either here in Soteria or some other beautiful destination. Nicole was taking summer classes, but that usually meant she would come up here to stay with everyone Thursday through Sunday.

"I'm doing great, but Jason's not here," I said.

There was silence on the other side of the phone for a few beats before she spoke again.

"He said he would be with you for a few weeks," she pressed, and I could hear the uneasiness in her voice.

"Yeah, he hasn't been here for over a month. Maybe there's some confusion with the dates?" I asked.

"Uh, maybe?" Mom said, but it didn't sound like she thought so.

"I'll call him, and then I'll call you back," I sighed before I hung up.

I tapped Jason's name on my phone and waited for him to pick up. After two rings, he picked up.

"Hey brother," Jason answered casually.

"Where are you?" I asked, getting straight to the point.

"Why?" he asked, and I immediately felt concern rushing through my body.

"Jason, Mom's freaking out. Where are you?" I demanded.

"I'm on vacation," he said.

"A vacation where?" I pressed.

"In Greece," he replied uneasily.

I paused at that. Why would he be there and not tell any of us? I heard footsteps behind me and saw Noah standing in the doorway with questioning eyes.

"Why the hell are you in Greece without telling anyone? That's dangerous, dude," I retorted.

Noah's eyebrows furrowed so deep that it looked almost painful. He mouthed the words *what, the,* and *hell* as I waited for Jason's response.

"I'm fine. I'm in a nice hotel overlooking some water right now," he said.

Now, I knew Jason worked part-time during the semester, but I was confused on how he afforded a trip like that without help.

"How did you afford that?" I asked.

"Dad," he said.

"What?"

"My dad, *not your dad*. He gave me some extra graduation money to celebrate," he continued.

"Uh, okay," I sighed.

"I promise we will talk about this more when I get back to the states in a couple weeks. I'll come up and talk about it. I just need you to trust me," he said.

"Yeah, okay," I replied uneasily.

"Just know that I wouldn't do this if I didn't have a reason," he said in a hushed voice.

"Okay, be safe," I groaned before he hung up.

"What the hell is going on? Why is he in Greece? What's in Greece?" Noah threw his arms out.

"I don't know. He wanted to talk about it in person." I shoved my phone in my pocket.

"The guy almost died. You would think he would know not to do stupid shit like this," Noah grumbled as he turned to go back in the house.

I watched as he walked back into the house. I wracked my brain as I thought about what my brother was doing in Greece. I prayed he was not looking for answers to something he was snooping into again. The first time he did this, he was looking for me, but what was it this time? There was nothing that came to mind.

My phone began to vibrate once again. It was my mother probably beyond worried. I went weeks in between speaking to her, but for her, Jason was different. I mean, she actually raised him. I tapped my phone to answer. It was a video call, and this time, she was there with the man I used to call dad. He smiled nervously.

"Hey Mom… Hey Dad," I said mainly to be nice because it would be weird to call him Mr. Westbrook or Jeremy.

"Did you get hold of him?" Mom asked anxiously before he could get any words in.

There was no way I was going to tell them the truth. It wasn't too often that I heard her get upset, but I knew she would. Plus, something in my gut told me not to. There were a few missing pieces to this complicated puzzle, and they definitely had something to do with things. I just couldn't figure out what and part of me was scared to put my all into finding out.

"Yeah, he's on some trip with friends from school in Europe right now. He said it's not too long, and then he'll be back here with me for a few weeks," I shrugged, trying to seem as nonchalant as possible.

There was silence on the other side of the phone. The only reason I knew they were still there was because it was a video call. They both looked at each other for a moment before turning to me again.

"Uh, where in Europe?" Jeremy asked, but for some reason instead of being concerned, he sounded uneasy.

"I… I don't know. I think he's going to multiple places," I lied.

"Oh, okay. Well, I wish he didn't worry me like that," Mom exhaled, and it sounded not as genuine as it could have.

"Yeah, well, you know Jason. Anyway, Mom, uh… Dad, he sounded fine. I'll talk to you guys later," I said.

"Okay, honey. I love you," Mom said.

"I love you too," I replied before I hung up.

When I got back inside, Noah looked at me expectantly. I shook my head as I sighed loudly.

"I don't know," I said.

"I don't think I will ever fully understand your brother," he rubbed his temples and I think we might have been in the same boat.

"Have you ever found Erica and Jeremy to be weird?" I asked Noah, which made him raise an eyebrow.

"I never thought about it. I barely speak to Erica, and I don't think I ever spoke to Jeremy. I mean, they seem nice. I know she loved Dad," Noah offered.

"Hmm, I don't know. I just feel like she knew I was alive all along," I said.

"Isn't there something called mother's intuition or something? Maybe that's why."

"But wouldn't that make you search for your kid?"

"I mean, maybe, but I think she also knew that it would be dangerous," Noah said.

"Maybe."

"If you really want to know, ask her." Noah shrugged.

Chapter 31

Rachel

It was the first time I was on campus since before Christmas. It was much more quiet than what I remembered, but the time of year was definitely to blame. It was summer, and there weren't even half the same amount of people there usually were during the fall and spring. I was happy to be back. I walked down a tree-lined path to the financial aid office and was happy to take in the cold rush of the air conditioner. I walked up to one of the counters that were free. The older lady sitting there smiled at me.

"Good morning. Can I help you?" she asked.

"Morning, and yes please. I want to make a payment on my account for the following school year," I said.

The woman smiled and clicked a few keys on her keyboard. She asked for my name and student ID number. I gave her the information, and she typed it in before her eyebrows went up high. I gave her a questioning look.

"What's wrong?" I asked.

"Nothing's wrong, but your tuition has been paid in full," she said.

"That's not possible. I didn't pay it," I countered.

"Well, maybe your parents did, sweetie. Aren't you lucky," she chastised, and I did my best to not roll my eyes at her.

Part of me wanted to shut her up by notifying her that both of my parents were, in fact, dead, so that would be impossible. I didn't though. She swung her screen around to show me that, in conjunction with scholarships, the thirty thousand dollars were paid. I thanked her and went back outside.

Feeling really confused, I picked up my phone and called Nicole. She answered after the first ring.

"Hey, I'm about to walk into class. Is everything okay?" she asked.

"Yeah, I'm fine. Did you pay my tuition? I told you I was going to Philly to visit and I would do it in person," I said.

"I remember, and no, I didn't pay for it… That's strange. Maybe Noah paid it? Sometimes he takes a look at the expense sheet and takes care of anything outstanding. Usually he says something, though. If it's not him, ask Josh," Nicole explained, very rushed, but I understood.

"Okay, thanks. Have fun in class," I said.

"*I won't.*" She chuckled before hanging up.

I tapped Noah's name on my phone, and he picked up after a couple rings.

"Ooh, Josh, it's your girlfriend," he answered, and I rolled my eyes.

"I'm glad that even after three months you still are as excited about it as we are," Josh replied dryly.

"Hey, you two, did either one of you pay my tuition?" I asked.

"No, I didn't," Noah said.

"Me neither, but I can if needed," Josh volunteered.

"No, I don't need you to. It's already been paid. I was hoping one of you had answers," I continued.

"That's weird. Is there some type of program or something for… uh," Noah hesitated.

"A "*my parents died in a fire*" fund? No I don't think so," I said, proud that I was able to speak about it now without getting emotional. My sense of sarcasm was slowly coming back. It sure as hell took long enough.

"Plus, if it was that, they would've told you. That's so bizarre. Did you see where the money came from?" Josh asked.

I hummed as I tapped on my phone to find the same page the lady showed of my account. When I got there, I was confused. I read what it said.

"International wire from Mykonos, Greece?" I read aloud, very confused.

There was silence on the other side of the phone. I could almost hear the sound of the wheels turning in their heads.

"What? What am I missing?" I urged.

"Jason is in Greece right now," Josh finally replied.

"Okay, I'm super jealous, but he wouldn't have thirty thousand dollars to just blow would he?" I asked.

"No, he shouldn't," Josh said.

"So, now I'm uncomfortable," I sighed.

"Ray, do you remember that situation way back last year with your car? We never got the chance to look into that further, but I wonder if they're related," Josh mused.

I did remember. My car's repairs were paid for twice. The plan was to investigate the matter more after the holidays, but then the fire happened. Our priorities had shifted. I wondered if someone else paid money to reverse what Tracey had planned to do.

Who was paying things? What were their intentions? I had no clue on who it could have been, but something told me I would find out more soon enough.

Author's Note

Usually, I use this space to thank everyone who has helped me over the past year. While I am truly grateful for those who cheered me on, whether it be reminding me that I would write a great story again or just reminding me to take some time away, this time I want to do something different.

This past year was full of changes for me. I started working full time after finishing my degrees. I fell in and out of love. I got sick and took longer than I ever had in my life to recover. All in which contributed to severe writer's block. Strangely enough, writer's block had never been an issue for me. I would stay up late at night mainly to get all the thoughts dancing in my head out on paper. This year was different and it was scary. I questioned my abilities and wondered whether I would be able to finish writing this book. Even after that, I was unhappy with the book and I rewrote many chapters several times. Trust me, there are many versions of this story, but only one will see the light of day!

Nothing worked for me until I finally gave myself time. I wanted *Burn* to come out in August like my previous books, but there was only one of me and hundreds of things to do. One of the most substantial gifts I gave to myself this past year was being kind. If you are a type A personality like myself, you know how it is when you have a goal. You set deadlines, you push your limits, and you get it done. I don't think I will ever *not* be that way, but I learned to be kind to myself. If I was tired, I would sleep. If I had things to get done the next day, I would write less and not force a thousand words out that day like I used to. The results came in slower, yes, but how can one expect to give to others when they were barely giving anything to themselves? It simply doesn't work.

I write this all to say that this book is a result of yet another year of growth and experiences; ups and downs; ebbs and flows. Life is forever changing and many times we have no choice, but to grow with it.

www.ingramcontent.com/pod-product-compliance
Lightning Source LLC
Chambersburg PA
CBHW051120190726
48290CB00006B/1610